GULL NUMBER 737

Gull Number 737

JEAN CRAIGHEAD GEORGE

THOMAS Y. CROWELL COMPANY

NEW YORK

BY THE AUTHOR

The Summer of the Falcon

My Side of the Mountain

The Hole in the Tree

Snow Tracks

Gull Number 737

Spring Comes to the Ocean

Designed by Albert Burkhardt

Manufactured in the United States of America

Published in Canada by Fitzhenry & Whiteside Limited, Toronto

Library of Congress Catalog Card No. 64-16531

ISBN 0-690-36171-8

3 4 5 6 7 8 9 10

TO LUKE GEORGE

CONTENTS

The Gull Chick

Luke Rivers watched the speckled egg in his hand. It was a simple thing, round, smooth, its gentle surface a restful shape.

He was leaning against a long, wooden table in a wind-swept sea house called the Sea Bird Lab. The laboratory was a shoestring operation headed by his father, Dr. Frank Rivers. Dr. Rivers sat backwards on a chair, looking closely at the egg in his son's hand. After a twenty-four-hour struggle, it had finally cracked. A small beak thrust out, then held still, as the nostrils drew in the first stream of air. The breath made the tiny gull chick quiet, and then energetic.

The Gull Chick

In a moment it had pounded a crack that ringed the egg.

"Does it hurt to be born?" Luke asked softly.

"I don't know if it hurts," his father answered, "but it's terrible to come from the hugs of a shell or a womb into air. But I guess no bird or beast ever really thinks 'Ouch, this hurts!' There isn't time."

Just then the chick made a strong swing at the shell and pierced a hole in it. An eye peered out at Luke. Like a camera, it took a picture on the brand new bird brain. The eye recorded a vaulting, beamed room, and a narrow table beneath a window. Chairs and filing cabinets were also recorded as well as maps and papers. Beyond that the bird eye printed a lonely, uninhabited beach and splashing ocean. But they were only photographs. They had absolutely no meaning for the chick.

The boy, however, was different. He moved. He was rounded. The bird felt "mother." The "mother" inspired him and he whacked his shell to make a bigger hole.

"Can I help him a little bit?" Luke asked. "His mother would, wouldn't she?"

"Not at the beginning. She can't help with this. She can incubate the egg, keep it moist, turn it over so it develops right . . . but she doesn't open the shell. The baby bird must do this alone." Then he added eagerly, "But I don't know why *you* can't help. Let's wait a minute and give him a chance."

Another patch of shell cracked away. A small, wet head wobbled into the air. Then another piece fell away, and another. Finally Luke's brown fingers uncovered from the round, simple egg a beautifully intricate herring gull. The chick flopped against Luke's warm palm, exhausted.

"I can't believe it," he said.

"I never do, either," replied his father. He pushed himself to his feet and touched the limp, wet chick admiringly.

"Look," Luke went on, "he has toes, and feathered shafts, nose holes; everything . . . and a minute ago he was just a round egg."

"And to think he started forty million years ago in the belly of some reptilian ancestor. See, he still looks like his ancestor with his beak and claws and no feathers. . . ."

The whistle of a jet from the Navy airfield across the bay interrupted his father. The plane came in low, and for a moment it was silhouetted black in the window. Its powerful engines shook the gray clapboard building.

Luke flinched and dropped the newly hatched sea gull to the floor. It gave a sharp peep and lay still.

"Oh, no!" he gasped, and swiftly scooped up the wet infant.

"Watch it!" his father snapped and pounced upon Luke's hands. "Is he all right?"

"He's still moving," Luke answered contritely.

"I'm sorry. That jet scared me. It was so quiet here with the birth of a chick."

Dr. Rivers glared at him.

"That's no excuse. It's so unnecessary to lose a chick out of carelessness. Now put him under your shirt and keep him warm—one breeze will kill him. Cover him up and let's just hope he isn't injured critically."

Luke pressed the tiny bird against his stomach as his father angrily walked to the window to close it. The wind from the mainland of Rhode Island hard-fisted the pane and then swept over the laboratory and far away. The Sea Bird Lab was quiet.

Luke was miserable. Finally he said, tentatively, "He seems all right, Dad. Do you want to test him?"

His father's first flare of anger had died. His fury was against carelessness, not against his son. His voice was no longer sharp when he said, "Let me see him. Is he dry?"

As Luke reached under his shirt he could feel the feathers and shafts that had looked like an old reptile's scales a moment ago. Now they were dry and tufted with fuzz. He took the soft, downy bird from his shirt and looked at it. The bird stared back at him. It trembled, and Luke felt a sudden compassion for the frightened new creature he had hurt almost before it knew what life was.

Dr. Rivers gently took the tiny gull from Luke's hand.

"Wide eyes in a sea gull means fear," he said. "I guess he's still a little shaken. But he must be hungry. So maybe he'll peck. I doubt that he's broken any bones." He turned the bird over on its back and the blue feet pumped the air for support. He examined the pot belly. It did not seem bruised. "We're lucky. He's okay."

"Poor chick," Luke said, and gingerly took back the baby gull.

His father stepped to the cabinet where his record cards were filed. He took out a fresh one and dated it June 5, 9:05 A.M. Then he studied a chart tacked to the wall of the laboratory entitled "Banded Birds." More than seven hundred birds were listed on the chart by date, number, and colors. The dates of entry went back five years, to the beginning of the sea gull study.

After checking the last number and colors used, Dr. Rivers picked from a box three expandable celluloid bands in a new combination of colors. He held the tiny gull's left leg firmly between his thumb and forefinger and snapped a blue, a yellow, and a green band around it.

Then he wrote down the colors on the record card. Next to the colors he jotted down the number of an aluminum band—737. He clamped this large band on the little bird. It hung loosely, for the band was designed for a full-grown bird. Next he wrote the number and colors on the chart.

"O.K., Luke, get the beaks ready," he said. "What shall we call him?"

Luke thought a moment, then with a sudden inspiration said, "Let's call him Spacecraft! He was frightened by a craft in space."

His father nodded. "Spacecraft is ready to go through the tests. Here, keep him warm in your shirt again. And get the cardboard heads, please. I'll get the tabulating sheets." He went to the filing cabinet. "I'm set," he said.

Luke opened a locker and took out seven cardboard shapes. One looked exactly like a herring gull's head, with a bright red spot under the lower bill. Another had a blue spot, the third had a green spot, and still another had a white spot on the lower mandible. One did not look like a sea gull head at all. It was square with a red spot on the lower side. The last was just a circle with a long pointed dart; it looked to Luke like a large lollipop. It, too, had a red spot on the lower side.

Luke reached under his shirt and gently drew out the gull. He placed him on the table. The tiny creature spread his webbed feet and stared around him. He was barely beginning to feel hunger pains; the food he had lived on in the egg still satisfied him.

Again the bird focused on Luke, the warm, moving "mother" thing. But nothing about the boy made him hungry. Spacecraft rested on his heels. Then he saw Dr. Rivers. That object did not make him feel hungry either, but as Spacecraft gazed upon one and then the other he felt a flicker of devotion and dependence.

"First, the mother head with the red spot," Dr. Rivers said in a singsong voice. Both father and son knew the order of the shapes, but his father always repeated them each time he ran a tapping test to be sure there were no errors.

The tests had to be run exactly the same each time they were made. Dr. Rivers was trying to find out whether the sea gulls of North America reacted in the same way as Dutch herring gulls three thousand miles away. In 1951, a Dutch ornithologist, Niko Tinbergen, had discovered that gulls react to very specific things and follow an unvarying pattern: a red spot on the parent's beak makes the young peck, the pecking then makes the mother or father gull bring up food from the gullet; the food is placed on the ground and gently fed to the babies. Tinbergen called the red spot a "releaser" because of the actions it triggered.

But Luke wondered just how many more times his father would have to make tests before he would be satisfied that North American gulls reacted in the same way as Dutch ones.

He held the first cardboard head above the chick. Here we go again, he thought to himself.

The Gull Chick

The white object above Spacecraft made him perk up. He had never seen a herring gull but some inherited instinct told him this shape was more exciting than the people he had seen. He stared hard at the red color.

Red, red, red, flashed through his eyes to his brain and back through his nervous system. Finally, he had to act. He lifted his head and swatted the spot dead center with a hard blow of his beak. He struck the spot again and again, not knowing why, only knowing he had to do what he was doing. Dr. Rivers counted the number of times and marked them under the heading "Red" in the first column on the tally sheet.

"You may be amazed by birth," he said to Luke, "but I never fail to be amazed by instinct. This little bird has never seen its mother. It has never seen another herring gull. It could not possibly know that pecking that spot makes the mother choke up food and feed it; and yet Spacecraft does it." He turned brusquely back to the business at hand. "Now the head with the blue spot, Luke. Snap it up!"

Spacecraft saw the head with the blue spot. He paused because blue did not send much of a message to his brain. But a spot was above him and it made his stomach ache a little. He had to do something to relieve his discomfort. Weakly, Spacecraft pecked the blue spot.

Dr. Rivers counted the weaker strikes and marked the card. He and Luke ran through all the tests. They saved the lollipop card with the red spot for the last. When the bird saw this card he pecked madly, harder than he had pecked at the model that looked like a gull's bill. Dr. Rivers sat forward in his chair counting and watching. Luke felt his own excitement rising. He watched the tiny bird as it finally sat down, confused and frustrated, and pulled its head close upon its shoulders.

"We're going to get the same results Tinbergen did," Dr. Rivers said. "The lollipop is the best releaser because it looks just like a parent gull to a chick." He paused at the window. "If you were a little gull in a nest you would look *up* at your mother; and she'd look like a lollipop with a red spot. That's why that shape gets the most whacks. The other shapes are side views of herring gulls . . . the way we see them. All of them get a reaction, no matter what color spot they have . . . but that's because the birds can see that there's a contrast. But it's the lollipop that makes a baby gull's mouth water."

Luke did not laugh at his father's old, tired joke. He'd heard it too many times before, just as he'd heard his father go over the familiar theories. Luke scooped up Spacecraft and put him under his shirt again to keep the little bird warm.

"Just think," his father continued, "the memory of a lollipop with a red spot is in the chick's mind when it's born! Wonderful, isn't it? Wonderful!"

Suddenly Spacecraft nipped Luke's bare stomach. Luke hollered in surprise and put him back on the table. The little bird looked up pertly. "Hey, stinker," Luke laughed, "quit that." Then Luke imitated the "mew" call of the mother herring gull. Spacecraft patted over to him like a toy on a string. Luke cupped his hands over the table, forming a little shelter, and called again. Spacecraft ran into the haven. He peeped contentedly.

Luke and his father chuckled.

"Shall I give the alarm cry?" Luke asked.

"Yes, let's see what happens."

Luke put Spacecraft in the middle of the table. "Hahaha" he cried, imitating a frightened gull. Spacecraft cringed. His eyes widened, his neck went down. Luke cupped his hands into a shelter again and called once more. Spacecraft ran swiftly under the shelter and crouched.

"He's scared to death," Dr. Rivers said. He picked up the fuzzy little bird and stroked its head affectionately. "You know, Luke," he mused, "we biologists have come full circle. I can remember when my father looked down on anyone who said a bear loved or a bird was afraid. He said it was reading human feelings into animals, which was absurd. He taught zoology and I can remember his tossing out one of my books that mentioned a fox that was 'sad.' In the nineteen thirties and forties David Lack and Franz Goethe, as well as Niko Tinbergen and Konrad Lorenz, began to come up with some amazing experiments that proved my little book right. Birds and beasts do 'feel,' much in the same way people do. Look." He held Spacecraft up to his eyes. "First we had a frightened bird, now we have a contented one. This is why we're out here, Luke—to find out how herring gulls live and feel."

He handed the chick to Luke, and continued, "Why, Ray Carpenter even proved that monkeys show compassion. He found that a troop of them swinging through the trees would slow down to let the old and infirm keep up with them. It's a nice thought."

Luke didn't want to hear any more. He was tired of listening and bored with his father's pet lecture about old ideas and new ones. "I'll take Spacecraft back to his nest," he said and started out the door.

His father nodded, and added, "See if you can get another chick. Gulls are hatching all over the gullery . . . and we can get a lot of tests done if we hurry. The more the better. Get along." He paused. "Hey, did you check the wall map to get the right nest?"

"No!"

"Come do it!"

The Gull Chick

Luke's irritation rose at his father's order. He stomped back. These eternal tests and all their details—would they ever end? He trudged into the big one-time living room of the rambling gray structure that was now the lab, and stood before an enormous map on the west wall. It showed the topography of the sand dunes. He studied it and wrote on a scrap of paper, "Rebel Club, Knoll A. Nest 7." Then he removed a red-headed pin that had been stuck in the map when the piping egg was brought into the lab. The pin told Luke where the egg belonged. Before his father had worked out this system, Luke had returned three chicks to the wrong nests, and the parents had killed each chick instantly. Gulls want no chicks but their own.

Next Luke took Spacecraft's 3 by 5 field card from the file. It also read "Rebel Club, Knoll A. Nest 7." "Check," he grumbled. He stuffed the field card back in the file, next to a lab card labeled "Spacecraft." On the lab card would be written wing and tail measurements, weights, reactions to tests—all the information that could be coded and given to an IBM programmer and finally a "think" machine. The machine would find out such things as the average weight of a two-week-old herring gull, or whether a one-day-old chick hits the red spot more or less times than a one-week-old chick. The field cards, on the other hand, were for notes about the birds in their natural world. Careful notations about food, when a bird learns to fly, and what they are doing at various times in various weathers would eventually give Dr. Rivers a day-by-day account of the life of the herring gull.

The gullery was just three hundred yards from the lab. The map Luke stood before showed the two groups, or "clubs," in which the gulls gathered to nest and raise their young. The gull societies were highly structured, and each gull knew its place within its group. The two groups waged such violent battles that Luke had named the first the Rebels and the second the Yanks.

There were about one hundred fifty nesting pairs in all, a small number for a gullery. Some gulleries on the mainland had two or three thousand birds. The smallness made the Block Island gullery ideal to study, for Luke and his father had been able to band almost all the bird members with both aluminum and colored bands. This was a great achievement; not many bird studies could boast such a record. In order to learn about club leaders and mated pairs it was necessary to know who was who; and the bands served this purpose.

Luke cupped Spacecraft tightly and started again for the gullery. He stood on the doorstep in the brilliant sunlight and squinted at the gray and black lighthouse on the tallest dune about a hundred yards away. Just beyond it was the gullery. Gulls were circling the lighthouse, crying and talking. They looked like tossed leaves as they soared. But Luke knew that this was not the aimless flying of leaves: each wingbeat, each cry, had meaning. After five summers of working with his father Luke felt that he knew more about gulls than he did about people.

"Hahaha—hahahaha," called a gull.

"Hahaha—hahahaha, yourself," Luke called back. "Yes, it's me. And you'd better warn everyone, Rebel girl, because I'm coming to the gullery whether you like it or not."

He unhooked a huge rubber mackinaw from a nail on the side of the house and put it on. It came to the top of his sneakers. He clapped on a pith helmet, large enough for two men. Then he started out across the sand. The gulls attacked anyone who trespassed on their nesting site, and they struck hard, so Luke never ventured into the gullery without the heavy armor his father had devised.

Luke felt Spacecraft struggling gently. He pressed the little bird closer, wondering what the terrible experience of being dropped at the moment he hatched would do to him in the days to come. Luke had heard his father say that birds often become conditioned to do something special under the stress of fear. He thought of the story of the crow that learned to talk when frightened.

Luke found himself speaking out loud to Spacecraft. "Will you always be afraid of the great spaces you'll have to fly in? Maybe you'll never fly for fear of being hurt. Or maybe being afraid so young will make you aggressive—a fighter. And then, someday you'll strike wings with the chief of the gulls and become the King of the Block Island gulls yourself!"

The birds began to gather above Luke as he took the trail through the grass to Rebel Hill. The long, lonely stretch of dune rolled against the horizon. The birds arose from their nests at his approach and came toward him. A gull struck his helmet, then hung above him, sculling the air and screaming. Luke plodded on. The bird tilted onto a wind and flew without flapping past the lighthouse to the lab. She called "Danger, danger!" to her mate.

Luke straightened his helmet and looked back. She was breaking her ride with flashing twists of her gray wings as she came to rest on the chimney of the Sea Bird Lab.

As he watched the bird alight Luke thought of his father. Every year Dr. Rivers passed up the opportunity to teach summer school at the college where he was professor of ornithology in order to accept a small National Science Foundation grant to investigate the herring gull (*Larus argentatus*).

Luke listened to the gulls scream louder and louder as he approached their nesting sites, and won·

dered why his father had picked the gull to study. It was not dying out like the whooping crane, nor was it eating crops like the blackbird. The herring gull was just a sociable bird, common and noisy.

But once Luke's father had made up his mind to study the gull, Luke's mother had joined the plan wholeheartedly. Summers on a sea island with two young children sounded ideal to her, even though the pay was small.

The first summer they drove from Columbus, Ohio, to Point Judith, Rhode Island, without stopping. Here they put the beach wagon on a ferryboat and steamed out into the Atlantic Ocean, several miles south and east, to the island. They docked at Old Harbor where the big wooden hotels sprawled, and where summer visitors fished from piers or went to sea in game boats. Block Island was a carnival spot, somewhat jaded and faded by time. But Luke and his younger sister, Eleanor, whom he had lovingly nicknamed Chinquapin after the pretty chinquapin tree, did not notice the tarnish. They saw only the grand buildings at Old Harbor and the charming farm houses set in the grass and bayberries along the roads.

After this first glimpse of the island, they were disappointed by the loneliness of the lab house. Luke still remembered their first sight of it. There were no trees on Block Island. The land rolled uphill to the south, and downhill to the north. Three miles along the only road to the north, the houses thinned out and fresh-water ponds filled every dip in the land. At the top of a hill far out on a lonely sand spit was a small gray house. Not even a road led to it. The beach wagon would be able to reach it only when the tide was out and the sand was packed hard by the waves.

The house had once belonged to an old sea captain. First it had been one big room with a fireplace—this was now the lab. Then a kitchen was added, then a bedroom off the living room, and lastly, a strange useless foyer. It was a scarecrow of a house, but to Dr. Rivers its charm lay in its closeness to the gullery where the herring gulls nested. He could eat his dinner and at the same time make notes about the beautiful white birds.

At first Luke thought it was fun to help his father study these big creatures of the sky. He remembered how excited and scared he had been that first day when his father had taken him into the gullery to trap birds. The big net had snapped like a mouse trap over fifty-two birds. Luke had plunged forward to help and, in his eagerness, had lifted the net too high and all but one bird—the largest—escaped. Over the flurry of wingbeats and cries, he had heard his father yell as he threw himself upon the last bird. The bird was terrified. Luke could see the glitter of its red-rimmed eye, wide with fear. The eye focused on Luke's father, and as it did, the bird opened its huge beak and the food in its stomach rolled upward in fear and desperation. The odor was overwhelmingly repulsive, but his father held on to the bird as he moved to a clean spot.

"Hand me the bands!" he had shouted. His grip had relaxed slightly, and the big bird swung his scissorlike bill around and clamped Dr. Rivers's hand. It began to bleed. The bird held on.

Luke was frightened now. "Let him go! Let him go," he screamed.

"Give me the bands!" his father cried furiously. "I'm all right."

Luke ran forward and gingerly handed his father an aluminum band. It was number one and on it was printed, "Please return to the Fish and Wildlife Service, Washington D.C."

His father finally managed to grasp the captive under his arm, belly upward. Being held on its back further terrified the gull. It opened its mouth to scream but no sound came out. All it could do was stare at the enemy that was forcing its heart to race at twice its normal speed. Luke watched the bird as his father placed the band around the right leg and clamped it shut. Then Luke handed his father a red plastic band. He snapped it around the left leg, but it was snappy and it pinched before he could adjust it. The bird struggled, and with an effort wrenched a wing free. The wing struck Dr. Rivers's face. Dr. Rivers carefully folded it back against the body. Finally, sweating under the strain of the whole procedure, he released the gull. The bird took one last frightened look at Luke's father, printed him on his bird brain forever, and flew off like an arrow.

"Wow!" Luke said. "This is rough business." He dropped onto the sand to watch the banded bird sail over the water. "We ought to give him a name. He's a humdinger." His father was on his knees watching the bird, too.

"He needs a great name," he said and wiped his forehead.

"Yeah, like *Larus argentatus,* his scientific name."

"Good! We'll call him Larus."

His father leaned over to gather the bands that had been scattered by the struggle. "That bird is going to remember me for a long time," he said. "I did a terrible job of banding him. But I guess I had to learn." He looked at his bleeding hand, and wrapped his handerchief around it. "These are powerful birds. I think I'll keep rubber bands in my pocket to put around their bills. And we ought to wrap strips of soft gauze around their bodies so they can't beat their wings and hurt themselves. Maybe we can keep them from getting so terribly upset."

For the rest of the week Dr. Rivers handled the birds deftly and gently, and by sundown seven days later he and Luke had banded 103 adult herring gulls. They were proud of the record.

Of all the birds, Larus remained special to Luke and his father, and they were surprised and delighted to find, after hours of observation, that Larus was the King of the Rebel Club.

But Larus did not return their fondness. Soon after the banding, Luke saw Larus sitting on a boat mast in Old Harbor. The red band shone brightly. "Hey, there's Larus!" he shouted. He and his father walked toward the big bird. Larus focused his gray eye first on Luke and then on his father.

"HAHAHA HAHAHAHA," he screamed and flew off.

"He remembers us!" Luke cried excitedly.

"He sure does," said his father, "and not very warmly, I'm afraid. That was a cry of hate—and fear."

Block Island's Gullery

Block Island lies off the tip of Long Island, south of Nantucket. Hurricanes strike it. Winds pile down on it summer and winter. The island is an outpost for weather warnings. It is twelve miles from the shores of Connecticut, four miles from the coast of Rhode Island. It is barren land, wind-beaten and rugged.

This island lay undisturbed in the Atlantic Ocean until 1661 when thirteen farmers sailed to its shores and settled there. In 1940 another group of settlers arrived on the island. They came by wing. Herring gulls floated down on the sand dunes and nested for the first time since the island was born.

These gulls had often summered on the island, catching skipper fish in the bright surrounding waters, but none had nested, for Block Island was far out in the sea and the vast shores of North America were big enough for all the sea gulls there were.

As the coast towns grew bigger and bigger, and people dumped their rubbish in piles along the ocean, or carried it to sea in barges, there was more food for the sea gulls. They visited the rubbish piles and went to sea with the garbage scows. This stretched their food supply of fish and mussels and clams. Their population exploded as the number of people exploded. Flocks of gulls winged up and down the blue-green coast.

Each flock had its own secret nesting spot on lonely dunes or isolated rocks. To these beloved grounds they returned in March to begin their ceremonial nesting season.

One year the gulls on the dunes north of Point Judith bickered for days. Nesting pairs found they had barely enough room to stretch. Although gulls like to nest side by side where they can mew and look at each other, they need at least seven square feet of land to live this close without arguing. Each couple had less than enough, and because they wanted more land, they kept placing their toes on each other's property. This would infuriate the owner and he would fight. Females quarreled with females, males choked in anger at males, some pulled grass—their sign of deepest rage—and many struck each other with their wings.

One dawn the gullery exploded into fury. Confusion and fear drove many birds high into the sky. In a matter of minutes the screaming sky of gulls had separated into two groups. One sunlight-splattered cluster circled and mewed over the Rhode Island dune; the other flew seaward.

The seaward colony followed their leader over the bay to the northern tip of Block Island where the sandpipers ran like shadows along the beach and the blackbirds twisted in the low bayberries as they expressed their spring love.

Above the dune the leader gave a long-drawn-out note. His beak was open, his neck was stretched forward and down. A plaintive sound to human ears, it did not sound sad to the tossing cloud of gulls. The note passed a sense of well-being through all the birds. Now they felt good toward the dune below them, the spit of sand that ran into the sea, and the green grass that leaned in the wind.

A stone lighthouse was below them. Two houses

were nestled in the blackberries a mile and a half from the tallest dune, and the village dump lay three miles to the south. The spot was awakening a feeling of property love in the birds. They circled it and circled it saying "Huoh" and "Mew," looking down at the cozy places behind clumps of green grass.

The leader dropped to earth. He alighted on the highest hill and, with his proud neck stretched as high as he could lift it, with his white feathers shining in the sun, he surveyed the domain. The gulls above watched him carefully.

Again he stretched his neck forward and downward. Again his bill was opened wide. Softly, he called the plaintive "Meeeeewwwwwwwwww." It said to his mate in the sky and the rest of the settlers, "I feel friendly toward my new territory, toward my mate, the nest I shall build, the young I shall raise. All's well."

Hearing this good call, a second male dropped onto the dune, then another and another, until the northern end of Block Island was settled with herring gulls.

About fifteen years—and many generations of gulls —later, visiting ornithologist Frank Rivers, Ph.D., walked the trailless stretch of beach to the lighthouse. He was watching the gulls. They led him straight to the gullery, and then he saw the odd gray-shingled house.

It was the answer to his dreams—a haven from a tiring year of teaching, and a place in which he could conduct his own study of herring gulls. His interest had been captured by the writings of Niko Tinbergen; he longed to explore the theories of the European bird behaviorists.

Dr. Rivers rented the rambling, primitive house and turned it into a lab. It was damp and gray. There were no light switches to flick. The furniture was old, but his wife loved the house on sight and it was not long before the children had taken it to their hearts.

The Leader
of the Gullery

That had been five summers—and many banded sea gulls—ago. Now on this sunny day in June, Luke Rivers was carrying a confused little gull chick to its nest. Spacecraft was the seven hundred and thirty-seventh gull Dr. Rivers had banded on Block Island.

The fluffy creature felt fear and hunger and strangeness all at once. His only comfort was the hand that pressed him to a warm belly. But the smoothness of the belly was not quite right. Some

ancient knowledge of what should be happening to
him began to make Spacecraft restless. The shirt
and hand and skin were wrong. The chick felt
nervous . . . and he scratched the stomach with his
hooklike middle claw.

"Ow!" Luke cried, "quit it!"

Luke hurried up the dune where the Rebel Club
gathered and nested. Deliberately he faced the lighthouse. The hummock to his right was Knoll A. He
walked three paces to the northeast and stood above
Nest 7. A red bit of cloth was tied to the beach grass
above it. This was one more precautionary act his
father made him take to insure the safe return of
nestlings.

Gently he brought gull 737 from his shirt. The
chick's feathers were moist and rumpled from Luke's
sweating fingers. Fear still held its eyes wide open, as
it made mental prints of every color and movement
in its view.

Spacecraft felt himself being lowered past grass
blades that flashed like green slides before his eyes,
past hot sand, into a yellow woven basket of grass.
The instant the gull chick touched the grass he felt
better. He shook and sat down on his heels, beside a
spotted egg. The wind blew and the hot sun took
water from the grass.

Luke was now in a whirl of white wings and
screaming birds. The parent gulls that had deserted

their nests at his coming had reconnoitered and were moving against him like an air force. They strafed closer and closer. But Luke was accustomed to their wings and went on with his work. He removed the red rag from the grass and walked among the nests looking for another new chick to test. In Nest 8 he saw a piping egg. He tied the red rag above it, wrote down the number and location of the nest, the Knoll, and the Club, then picked it up.

Suddenly his pith helmet spun off and a foul odor assailed him. The parents of Spacecraft had returned, and recognizing Luke as their enemy, struck him on the head. They vomited old food all over his slicker. Luke grimaced as he realized he was now receiving the gulls' expression of their most deeply felt rage and hatred.

Sea gulls regurgitate as an expression of love when they court each other, and they choke up food to feed their young. Lovely as the habit is to them, they also know this act is repulsive to enemies. Over the aeons they have driven off foxes, raccoons, weasels, snakes, and humans with the contents of their stomachs.

Through with Luke, Spacecraft's mother swung about and kliooed to her chick. Spacecraft heard his mother call. Not knowing who she was or why he cared, he sat up and looked about brightly. She came to him; her white wings hung above him. Dropping lightly, his mother stood delicately on the nest. "Klioo," she said gently. Glancing around to make sure no enemy was in sight, she stood over him. Spacecraft saw her red spot and knocked it so hard her beak jerked upward. Her throat began to swell, her eyes softened, and without sound she stretched out her neck and placed food on the ground beside the nest. The sight of food, his mother, the nest—all the right things—made Spacecraft open his beak. His mouth was so enormous that his mother could see all the way down his pink gullet to the dark empty stomach. This sight awakened a terrible need in her and she began to poke morsel after morsel of food into the warm throat.

Finally the bill could not open for another bite. The chick blinked sleepily, wobbled, and sat down. The young mother herring gull stepped over the downy nestling and gently sat on it. She fluttered her wings, wiggled her tail, and tipped her eye proudly to see the bulge in her breast feathers that jutted out over her wonderful sleeping chick.

At the bottom of the dune Luke stopped to wipe his foul-smelling helmet in the grass. Five summers of this had made him so accustomed to the insults of the gulls that it was hardly more than an annoyance. Then he heard a nestling peep on Rebel Hill. He glanced up the dune and wondered what hatched youngster he had missed. He started up to find it, thinking that his father could test it while they waited for the piping egg to hatch. He scrambled up the dune again, feeling the bird in the egg thump to get out. Spacecraft's mother was frightened by his sudden appearance and reluctantly left her nest again.

Suddenly another Navy jet screamed over the island. With an ear-splitting sound, it sped by a little south of the gullery.

Luke stopped while the sound filled the air, and sensed something was wrong. His eye was attracted to Spacecraft's nest. The little fellow flopped strangely and crouched. Luke walked over to him. Poor thing, he thought. Perhaps Spacecraft is confused, with first a boy for a mother and then a bird . . . perhaps . . . but Luke stopped guessing. His father had taught him to write down all observations. Eventually, many, many notes and hours and days and times would tell the story. It took much more than one observation and several guesses to know what bird behavior was about.

Luke was glad he had his notebook with him. He often resented his father's insistence that he never go to the gullery without it, but this time he could see his father's wisdom. He would have forgotten the details by the time he got to the lab. He wrote down the date and the time. Then he noted: "Spacecraft returned to nest. Mother accepts him; but Spacecraft terrified. Eyes wide, feathers flattened . . . im-

mobile. All the signs of fear in a gull. No reason.
No hawks around, just me, and a Navy jet passing to
the south."

He put away his pencil and hurried down the
curve of the dune.

The next morning Luke hummed as he returned
home from the gullery. There were two chicks under
his shirt, and the sun was out. He watched his sister
Chinquapin pass the lighthouse wearing her usual
rig—sneakers, blue jeans, and a bright-colored shirt.

He called to her. "Hey, where are you going?"

"To Old Harbor," she answered.

Something in her grin alerted him that she was
up to mischief.

"What for?" he demanded, as she halted im-
patiently.

"To see Ginny," she said with finality. Ginny was
the daughter of Captain Gregory, the lobster fisher-
man, and was Chinquapin's close summer friend.
Then his sister squinted her eyes and looked at him
conspiratorially. "I'll tell you what I'm going to do
if you promise not to tell," she said.

Luke's promise was firm. "I won't."

"I'm going to get a job."

"A job!"

"Yes." Chinquapin put her hands on her hips
and flounced her head. "I am tired of pretending

31

that learning and pursuits of the mind are more important than pretty things. I'm tired of Dad contributing to 'world knowledge' while I have to wear last summer's bathing suit."

"Chinquapin! What are you saying?" Luke looked aghast at his little sister. This was an unexpected outburst.

"You know what I'm saying. You've said it, too. You wanted to go West with the Outdoor Club this summer and work on that ranch . . . but all you got was, 'Now, son, money is not everything.' "

Luke stared into the impudent face. She had touched a sore spot, and a hot sword of anger stuck in his throat as he remembered the scene with his father. He had asked if he might go on a camping trip to the West with his high school Outdoor Club. It would be a marvelous summer. They would work on a dude ranch for room and board. Luke had wanted desperately to be a part of the adventure, but Dr. Rivers had said no.

Luke had begged.

His father had looked superior. "We have a wonderful place on an island in the sea with water and wind and boats . . . and you're not satisfied. You want to go somewhere else. What other boy of sixteen has the chance to work on a sea island on a real research project?"

Luke had wanted to shout at him, "I'm tired of gulls. I want to be with my friends," but his father was too stern.

"I thought you enjoyed the gulls and the Sea Bird Lab." his father said in a tone that admitted no rebuttal.

Hurt, confused, and afraid to speak out his real feelings, Luke said slowly, "I do. I do." But in his heart he hated the gulls, the tedious hours of work they required, and the lonely, lonely lab at the end of the sandspit.

Suddenly Luke realized that Chinquapin was staring at his hurt. He was angry at her for seeing; and he was angry at her for being free to do what he could not do.

"Money, money," he shouted in wrath, "you're always thinking of money!"

"It's not so sinful," she said with a flip of her chin. "A girl has a perfect right to earn money if she wants to." She turned and walked haughtily away, her sneakers digging hard in the shifting sand.

Luke watched her go. She did not glance back, but ran to the top of the lighthouse dune, then she took a big leap and disappeared from sight.

"Nuts!" he said out loud. Painfully he remembered the exciting job that had been offered to him the day they arrived this summer. Ginny's father,

Captain Gregory, had asked Luke if he would like to help him string bait-fish and set and lift lobster pots. The paycheck could add up to $35 or $40 a week, depending on the weather. The offer was just what Luke wanted since he had to spend the summer on the island, but he knew better than to ask his father. Dr. Rivers would say no, and then tell Luke again how lucky he was to be doing research. So he had postponed giving Captain Gregory an answer, hoping that if he and his father finished the demanding bill tests, he would have some free time to work. Captain Gregory had said afternoons and weekends would be all right.

Luke had not been back to give the Captain an answer. He and his father had been too busy. Now, Chinquapin was off to wait tables in a hotel or clerk in a gift shop—something—and he was green with envy. If she could do it, he certainly should be able to.

His dark mood stayed with him as he worked through the morning. He helped his father color-band and test fifteen hatching chicks. Dr. Rivers's spirits rose as chick after chick reacted to the cardboard heads. But even a good lunch failed to cheer Luke.

By two o'clock the day's work was done. All the chicks were returned. Now, thought Luke, I'll see if I can think up a scheme to get away. He had decided to make the plunge. He would make an arrangement with Captain Gregory and then tell his father.

Dr. Rivers sat down at the lab table to study the results. "Fascinating!" he said.

Luke was tired. He sprawled beside his father, head on his arms. Pots and pans were clicking in the kitchen as his mother, returned from the store at Old Harbor, began to prepare supper. Luke heard her humming. His father began to hum, too. Luke lifted his head, listening for Chinquapin's footsteps. She had not returned for lunch, and Luke was holding back her secret out of sheer will power.

His father was smiling. Tentatively Luke approached him.

"Dad, may I take the boat? I'll get some notes on loafing sea gulls. The other day you mentioned that all the sitting around they do ought to be studied."

"Yes, do," his father replied, looking up briefly from his notes. "There is nothing in the literature on loafing. And gulls spend half their time doing nothing . . . that's fine. And one of these days you might pick one bird and follow it—time him from dawn to dusk."

Luke was relieved to see his scheme had worked. He felt a little guilty about not being entirely honest. Still, he could get some notes on the banded birds and make arrangements with Captain Gregory, too. He jumped into action.

How Dad does love his work, Luke thought. It really is a little contagious. It would be nice if he would study boys as closely as he studies gulls.

Outside, Luke looked toward the lighthouse. The birds circled gently in their tightly structured world, calling to their young, keeping clear of any neighbors, guarding their homes.

He slipped around the edge of the house and jumped over the bayberries to the beach. To his right the narrow point stretched into nothing. It was white with the explosion between the waves that ran in from the Atlantic and those that ran out from the bay. They met with loud booms and high splashes over the tip of Sandy Point.

The family motor boat was high on the beach. Luke put his shoulder to it and was shoving it toward water when a gull alighted on the bow.

"Git!" he shouted. The bird's bands shone Orange-Blue. Luke remembered him clearly; he was a member of the Yank Club. Orange-Blue stretched his neck, opened his beak, and "hahaed" at Luke. Obviously the gull remembers me too, Luke thought. Probably scared when we netted him. It seems they never forget that fear. With a jolt the boat hit the water, the bird lost his balance and floated on the air.

Luke jumped in and started the motor. It roared, the craft lurched into the waves, and Luke shouted,

"Wheee!" It was a relief to get away from the demanding work. He steered the boat around the spit into the Bay of Cows. He was followed by the gull with the Orange-Blue leg bands.

At the edge of the bay the gull was joined by his mate. Luke wondered why. It was nesting time, and one of them should be home guarding the nest. But he shook the thought away. He didn't really care, he was off to "life"—noise and people and work. He hummed and gunned the engine.

Now he was on the eastern side of the island just opposite the gullery. Three more miles along the sandy State Beach and he would be at Old Harbor. He could see people swimming close to shore, and he felt cheered. The two gulls above him dropped low and rode the air currents created by the boat. Luke glanced at them with annoyance. He glanced again. The male had his head turned and was staring at him.

Oh durn, Luke said to himself. I can't help but like these crazy critters. I hate 'em and love 'em. He slowed the boat down. The gulls slowed down. He couldn't stop being curious about them.

They were a young couple that had only been mated that year, so they did not have much status and were forced to nest at the edge of the group in a very insecure spot.

Something's happened to their nest, Luke mused. Something has killed the young . . . now, I wonder. . . .

A large gathering of gulls dropped down to loaf beyond the waves in front of the Public Beach house. Luke counted them, noted the time, and made a few hasty observations. Orange-Blue and his mate had dropped onto the water beside him and were bobbing high and cork-like. All the gulls seemed peaceful. Luke noted the fact on his clipboard. Then he picked up his binoculars and studied the group. The boldest held their heads higher than all the rest. Luke thought it was like having a policeman on the corner of the block. They seemed to keep order among the resting birds. He noted that also.

Suddenly Orange-Blue and his mate lifted themselves heavily on their wings and took off. Luke watched them go. He felt he ought to follow them— and find out what had become of their young.

But he wanted to get to Old Harbor.

He headed for the port. As he came in between the breakwaters that jutted into the sea he thought he saw Ginny and Chinquapin at Captain Gregory's lobster shack. Docking, he saw no girls, but there above him on the flagpole of the shack sat Larus, the King of the Rebels, the first bird ever banded on Block Island.

Luke climbed out onto the boardwalk. He ran

lightly toward the lobster shack, keeping his eye on the splendid Larus.

Captain Gregory's boat was not in. Luke's spirits fell and he kicked the air in disappointment. He had counted on seeing the Captain. Swallowing his disappointment, he walked over to stand under Larus.

"What are you doing here at this time of day?" he called to the preening bird. "You should be over at the dump with the rest of the Rebels." There were other gulls on the roof of the shack and on the empty storehouses beside it. Luke read several of their bands and wrote them down. His spirits picked up as he went on observing the birds.

What a bunch of loafers, he thought to himself. Why were they here today? No lobster boats were in with trash fish. And then he saw Abnormality, the character of the island. Luke was fond of the old beachcomber and happy to see him at this moment. It was Tuesday, and as he did every Tuesday, Abnormality was feeding the gulls the scraps he had gathered all week from the hotels. The smiling man with his far-off blue eyes was dressed in his usual dingy white coat and pants. He sat on a piling, talking to the gulls and throwing them food. Luke realized that Larus had finished eating—he had eaten first because he had outmaneuvered the other males and had now retired to his sitting post to let the other members of his club eat. He was perched high, ready to call a warning if he saw a gull from the rival group.

Luke stood and watched Abnormality for a few minutes. The old man's carefree expression made Luke forget his own disappointment. Abnormality was swinging his legs and making "mew" sounds— "all's well," in gull language. Beside him rested Polly, his pet pig. Luke tried to recall whether he had ever seen Abnormality without Polly. He could not. The two shared an old stone ice house not far from Captain Gregory's shack on the wharf, and as far as Luke knew, both had lived there forever. Abnormality walked the beaches with Polly and gathered mussels or fished for pollocks. He was not mentally with the world. He told people he lived in a shack and scrabbed off the seashore because he had the power to make ill people well again. If he worked, he said, the power would go. Abnormality could recall cases where he had healed presidents and governors and great singers. Unfortunately, since he happened to be the only person around at the time, his claims remained unproven.

But his queerness made no difference to the people of Block Island. When life seemed too competitive and tough they would think fondly of Abnormality living his simple life and wish they had his tranquillity. His very gentleness made other people more serene when they saw him, and the islanders would let no visitors make fun of him.

Luke walked up to Abnormality. "Hi, Abnor, how are the sea gulls?"

"Free and wild and feathery," Abnormality answered absently as he tossed out shingles of bread.

"What's Larus been up to?" Luke pointed to the bird gleaming white and gray in the sunlight.

"Larus? Larus?" Abnormality's eyes clouded and he shook his head. "He will soon be dead. I can not heal him anymore. There is another bird that eyes him greedily. He will soon be president."

Luke chuckled, for Abnormality made up all kinds of tales about the gulls. It gave him a chance to come to the Sea Bird Lab and talk. He was convinced that Dr. Rivers and Luke were the only other sane people in the world because they, too, talked to birds.

Luke scrutinized the splendid gull, and then remembered his sister. He was curious about whether or not she had found a job. "By the way, have you seen Chinquapin?"

Abnormality nodded. "I saw her," he said.

"Where?"

"I'm not gonna tell you," he answered smugly.

Luke shrugged and wandered back to the lobster shack. There was still no sign of Captain Gregory; the boat was still out. A wave of disappointment swept over him again. He'd just have to find time tomorrow.

Luke returned to his boat and went all around the island, counting the loafing birds, trying to see which gulls loafed on the waters and shores to the south and which used the western beaches. The sun was bright and the bands were hard to read. He concentrated hard for several hours before he circled home.

Disappointed not to have found the Captain, but satisfied that he had achieved what he told his father he would, he beached the boat, stretched, and looked down the sandspit. Three hip-booted men were casting their lines at the end of Sandy Point. Luke wished he could join them.

He heard a grunt behind him and wheeled around to see Abnormality again. Abnormality had walked the miles from the harbor to the spit, leading Polly on the leash. "Wait for me!" Abnormality called. The foam twinkled around his bare feet.

Luke waited.

"Are you and your father going to Boston this summer to see your gulls?" Abnor asked.

Luke remembered that during each of the past summers, he and his father had gone to Boston and Cape Cod to look for birds they had banded. His father wanted to know how far the birds born on Block Island wandered when they returned from the winter migration. The data were showing that most young gulls tend to come home to their ancestral nesting grounds. However, as in all his father's researches, records from three years were not enough proof. So Luke was sure they would again go to Boston this summer. He nodded his answer.

"Then you must take me!"

Luke raised his eyebrows. Abnormality had never been off the island in his life. He studied the man's tanned face. "Do you mean that?"

"Yes, I do. I mean that. I also mean take me to the airport. I shall fly like a bird to the city of Chicago."

"Are you serious, Abnor?" asked Luke. "Why on earth do you want to go to Chicago?"

Abnor picked up a clam and put it in his pocket.

"I'm supposed to meet a doctor there. He's gonna help me."

"Help you what?"

"Help me . . . I don't know . . . he's very famous. He can cure, just like me. But he can cure folks and keep a job. You see, I've never been able to do that. If I go to work my healing powers will be taken away. But now, this famous man will show me how it's done. Then I can work and heal. I can do both."

"I see," Luke said, but he didn't. The cries of the gulls mingled with his thoughts.

"Will you take me?"

"Well," said Luke, stalling for time, "do you have the money?"

"I have a ticket." Abnormality pulled an Airways Airline ticket from his pocket.

Luke examined it with a frown. It was quite real.

"The man in the travel agency at the hotel will fill in the date when you say when."

"I'll tell you when," Luke told him gently.

"Thanks."

His mission completed, Abnormality's attention turned away. He squatted down and took the clam from his pocket and placed it on a stone. He smashed it with a blow from another stone, then, standing, he shouted "Klioo" into the wind. A sharp-eyed gull passing over saw the clam, braked with his wings, and plunged to Abnor's side.

Luke left them and turned toward the lab. He wondered what was in store for Abnor and who had sent him the ticket.

Abnor called after him in a nice voice, "Now I'll tell you where Chinquapin is."

"Fine," laughed Luke. "Where is she?"

"She's on Captain Gregory's lobster boat . . . lifting pots . . . working with Ginny."

Luke froze in his footsteps. Slowly, in pain and disbelief, he turned around to make sure he had heard the truth. But Abnormality was talking to the gull.

With a shove, Luke put the motor boat back in the water, pulled the starter, and opened the gas lever wide. He left it there all the way back to Old Harbor.

The lobster boat was in. Luke tied up, vaulted to the pier, and ran to the shack.

"Chinquapin!" he cried as he reached the lobster house. His sister, wrapped in an oilcloth apron, was threading smelly trash fish on stringers. Ginny, beside her, was also stringing fish. Both girls stopped and wiped their sweating faces with their arms.

"Hi!" Chinquapin laughed. "I'm working. We were out on the boat all day. Now we're getting bait ready for tomorrow . . . and, oh, Luke the lobsters are e-n-o-r-m-o-u-s!"

Luke was so stunned and jealous he could only be angry. "How can you! Dad'll be furious. That's terrible, smelly work for a girl."

"Cheer up. We only do this one day a week. If we get all these done and in those barrels," Chinquapin pointed, "then we can spend all the rest of the week baiting and lifting the lobster pots. And, on Saturday—money, a new bathing suit, and red shoes! No more scuffed old pumps!" She lifted her shoulders in laughter. "Come on in, the smell's fine!"

Luke clenched his teeth and watched Chinquapin push hard at a tough scaly fish, poke the needle through with a burst, and make a knot. She tossed the stringer into a barrel. Her eyes flashed defiantly.

"It's no worse than wearing that hot old slicker and pith helmet and going into the gullery to have birds choke up all over you."

"I won't tell on you," Luke retorted, "but I'd sure hate to be in your shoes when Dad finds out." He spun around and left in a white heat of fury.

His mother was taking a lamb stew from the stove that evening when Chinquapin pushed open the cloth screen on the back door. Chinquapin's hair was wet, her cheeks pale. Her face was lined with tiredness.

"I'm weary, but wealthy," she announced and staggered dramatically to her chair.

"Where've you been?" he father snapped. "You've been gone all day."

"I've been out stealing," she teased.

Dr. Rivers's face remained expressionless. Luke was fascinated. He envied the way Chinquapin could handle his father. Chinquapin moved right into the battle.

"Daddy, you're an angry gull," she said firmly. "Your eyes are wide and your feathers are flat. All right, I'll tell you." She pulled her neck down to her shoulders and whispered. "Now you can't strike me. I'm a humble sea gull child who comes to her parents with her neck in so she won't get hit."

Dr. Rivers began to smile.

"You know too much," he said. "Come on, humble gull child, tell me what you've done."

"I went to work. Me, your subdominant chick."

"Subdominant!" Luke exploded. "Wow! you have all the dominance and grit of Larus, plus your own human intelligence."

"Hush," his father said. "This is between your sister and me." He turned to Chinquapin. "Where are you working? What's this job?"

"I'm a lobster lady," Chinquapin said. She raised her head and looked her father in the eye.

"Watch out, little gull chick," Luke warned, "your head is higher than your father's, and you know what happens then. . . ."

But his father ignored him. Dr. Rivers spluttered, "You're a what?"

His mother rose from the table and cried, "Eleanor Rivers! I will not have it. I will not. That's heavy work."

"And smelly," added Luke with relish. "You should see the trash fish she has to string."

Chinquapin blazed at her parents, "Oh you! You want me to be a nice little girl, a lovely, lovely lady, and yet I can't even have red shoes for my feet. Why? Because we're so darned intellectual that these frivolous things are not for us. We're superior to red shoes and new fashions and silly music; but not because they aren't wonderful, only because we can't afford them." Her voice was becoming shriller. "Well, that's not for me. I have a job . . . and I'm going to keep it." She fled from the table and grabbed the wooden banister that led to her half-an-attic room above the kitchen.

"Come back," her mother said sharply. "Now wash your hands and eat your supper. I want no more nonsense." The family silently started to eat.

"Lobstering should be fun," Dr. Rivers finally said. And then he added with enthusiasm, "I have Hegner's book on *Invertebrate Zoology*. Would you like to learn more about lobsters? Perhaps you could help Captain Gregory increase his business. . . ." His store of knowledge sent him into action, and his mind was already leaping beyond the problem at hand. He rose and went to his library and found the book. He read aloud to them about lobsters—*Phylum Arthropoda*—as he walked back to the table.

Luke leaned over his stew. He had no interest in it. Why? why? he cried to himself. Why does he let Chinquapin do what she wants . . . and I have to take directions like a child? Anger was rising in him. He pushed his plate away and rose and went quickly to his room. If I were a sea gull I'd pull grass, he muttered to himself.

On the Sand Dune
of the Gulls

Larus, the great sea gull, opened his eyes when the light of dawn set off an inner trigger. He stared at the blue sands of morning. The ocean and sky were one wet arch of shimmering mist. No other bird was awake on the gullery. He could see the sleeping humps that were his neighbors; their heads were tucked into the feathers of their backs, their bodies balanced on one foot. The dune was white with them. Larus lifted his feathers and lowered his foot slowly.

When he had a firm two-footed base, he shook. Then he contemplated his feet. All sea gulls contemplate their feet. Cats purr, dogs wag their tails, but sea gulls stare at their feet. No one but a sea gull knows why.

The bird lowered his head. He sounded a soft "Mewwww" from his hill. Like an echo, the chief bird across the ravine on Rebel Hill answered back, his neck forward and down, his bill wide open.

Another gull awoke and also mewed. Two others called. The gullery stirred. Birds flapped their wings and defecated. Nestlings looked up and tapped the red spots on the underside of their parents' beaks, but there was no food to be choked up, for the food of the day before had been consumed to maintain the high metabolism of the birds during the night. The parents preened their back feathers to make them airtight. While they waited for the sun to heat the land and make warm breezes rise, they straightened the under covert feathers that acted like brakes and wing flaps in flight.

One female, still brooding her downy young, suddenly felt kindly toward her mate. She picked up a piece of old food and placed it affectionately deep in his throat. As she did, his feathers lifted, making his eyes soft and warm and his body big. He stood closer to her. But their breeding time was done. There were other things to do. The male stared at his wobbly young and his warmth for his mate died. He had to gather food.

The light grew a few degrees brighter, awakening all the birds on the gullery. A handsome white-footed gull stood quietly on his sandy sleeping spot and stared at his mate who was turning her three eggs so the growing chicks would not rest too long in one spot. Development depended on this. One egg rolled back. She eyed it and shoved it with her beak once more. It stood on end for a moment and then rocked into position. She sat down ever so gently. Beside her a female called "Mew." The females had rounder heads and their eyes were lower than the males. This gave a softness to their faces, the only outward difference between a male and female herring gull.

Preening took fifteen minutes in the morning, half an hour at noon, and twenty-five minutes in the late afternoon, plus a few touches during the day. The birds depended upon an immaculate, water-repellent covering. It was not grease that kept the water out but good grooming. They all had an oil gland on their bodies, but its purpose was to keep their beaks from breaking and splitting, not for oiling their feathers.

Another female was lifting the tiny feathers at her neck. Her eyes closed as she snapped the barbs of the feathers together by running her beak through them. When the barbs were locked, they strengthened the

vein. This strength was the difference between float-
ing and sinking on water, and was responsible for
effortless flight in the sky.

Now that the light was high, it was time for Larus
to relieve his mate and sit on their three eggs. He
walked, head high, to his partner of five years and
looked in the nest. It was empty. He didn't know
what to do; his eggs had mysteriously disappeared.
His mate saw they were gone, too, but sat down
anyway. The pattern of sitting was deeply ingrained
in her being. She got up again. She swished her tail
and sat down. She rose and walked away. The empty
nest confused her. Her instincts told her to do one
thing, her brain told her to do another.

Larus contemplated his feet. He did this for many
minutes. Finally his mate came over to him. Softly she
said "Klioo." Her neck was outstretched, her head
down. She begged food from Larus. In sea gull
language this meant "I love you." Larus felt gentle.
He stretched himself as high as possible and made
himself large and handsome. His eyes were bright.
He looked for some male to challenge to a game of
grass pulling or neck stretching. None would take
him on.

His mate walked around him once more, softly
calling "Klioo." Larus walked a few feet to the edge
of his territory and surveyed his land.

She tossed her head. Larus liked this. He led her

to another corner of their land and pretended to build a nest.

Suddenly his female walked away. Larus followed her. Then she turned and begged food like a baby gull, for the skills of love are closely tied to the earliest movements of the birds. Larus tossed his head. She tossed hers. With a strong, pulsing rhythm, Larus and his mate tossed heads, his moving higher and higher, until she saw nothing in the world except him. She bowed her head. Larus flashed open his great sunny wings and flew to her back, his feet on her shoulders.

His female touched her beak to his breast. Larus cried out two low notes as he stretched his head forward. He called three high notes, head down. A final loud scream pierced the air as Larus trumpeted the call of the mating herring gull.

A moment later he winged to his sand throne on the dune. He stared across the waves toward the morning feeding grounds of the Block Island gulls. The sand was warming, heating the air. The breeze began to rise. It bent the beach grasses. It came up the dune. Larus opened his wings and air rose under them, lifting him off the ground. Bow-winged, he sailed up and backwards rising higher and higher with the onshore wind. Suddenly the breeze from the west struck one from the east. The turbulence of the meeting forced Larus to flap to stay steady. He beat hard as he sailed over to Cormorant Cove where the ebbing tide was exposing a pantry of mussels and clams.

He felt his mate behind him. She had taken the same breeze and was following devotedly to the feeding ground. There were no eggs to incubate, and she was not quite ready to lay again.

The past week had been a sad one for Larus and his mate. Their eggs were almost ready to hatch, when a snake broke two and made off with the remaining one. Patiently his mate began nesting again, laying one egg each morning for three days. Then one of these disappeared on Monday. She did not lay another as a chicken does when the farm wife takes her eggs; instead she incubated two eggs. But the next morning one of those disappeared, and finally this morning the third was gone.

Now on this blue misty morning she had mated again. In a few hours there would be another egg.

Larus alighted on the yellow and brown sea weed that stretched like ribbon along the mussel-covered shore. With his powerful beak he wrenched a mussel from its fibrous mooring.

All gulls love hard objects. No sooner are their beaks around a clam shell than something wonderful happens inside them. It was happening to Larus. He felt the urge to climb in the sky. He did not even wait for a wind to help him go aloft, but beat his wings way up above the beach. When he was high, he dropped the mussel. It smashed onto the rocks at the edge of the sea. Larus dropped down to eat the sweet meat.

His mate also dropped a mussel. It struck the sand and did not break. She alighted beside it, picked it up, and carried it into the sky. She dropped it three more times before she hit a rock.

Larus and his mate dropped mussels for about an hour. Other gulls came to the shoals, but only one other pair. The rest were single gulls. It was the height of the nesting season and they were taking turns at brooding and guarding their eggs or downy young.

The other pair at the shoals were Orange-Blue and his mate, the birds that Luke had seen on the other side of the island the day before.

Presently the gulls who had young returned to the gullery. One female had to peck her mate to get him off their chicks. The urge to sit and protect them was so great that it often took a prodding to make one of the parents stop. The male shook and got ready to hunt. The female walked to her chicks to hover over them. The chicks saw the red spot. Jab, jab, jab, the beak of the female was knocked so hard it made her head jerk. Her whole being responded. The food she had gathered formed a soft ball and it rose in her neck. She made a few rippling movements and deposited it on the ground. The thumping chicks hopped and flopped and opened their beaks. She saw the red gullets, wide and cavernous. Gently she picked up the morsels from the sea and pressed them far down into the little mouths. The chicks swallowed with guzzling sounds, wobbled, rocked, and closed their mouths.

Larus and his mate were still on the mussel shoal. She leaped to a rock. He followed. They were filled with food and pleasantly quiet. Larus preened his under covert feathers. The ride over had not been as smooth as it might have been. He felt a need to check his pinnings. Softly his mate called "Klioo." She begged. Larus felt gallant once more and he lifted his feathers with affection. He was going to whack a male that had alighted near them, when his mate suddenly stretched her neck. Her eyes widened, her feathers flattened. The egg was pressing within her. She spread her wings and flapped swiftly over the Coast Guard station, over the breach where the New London ferryboat entered the western harbor, and down the Logwood Cove. She tilted and tipped as she fought the winds all the long way to the gullery.

Larus watched her for almost a mile, so keen were his eyes and his feelings for his mate. He knew her from every other bird in the gullery even at a great distance.

When she winged out of sight, he hopped a wind

over the island and followed her home. He passed seven young males from the Rebel Club sitting on the harbor light gazing toward the United States. They were waiting for the ferryboat. There would be scraps of food for the gulls from the kitchen. Larus paid small attention to them.

He swept home to see his mate on their nest. She arose and looked into the warm grass. A round egg lay there, speckled and wet. She rippled her neck and sat down again. Larus preened.

An hour later he was flying around above the nest when he flattened his feathers and widened his eyes. His mate reacted immediately. He was afraid, so she was afraid. She wanted to fly away, but she was held to the nest by the egg. Confused, she lifted her wings.

"Hahaha—hahahaha," Larus cried.

This was too much. She pumped her wide wings and lifted herself safely above the ground. But she stayed above her nest, anxious that the egg might disappear. She called, "Kleew klew," which means "I am here," and Larus answered "Kleew klew."

Larus had seen a burlap dome in the beach grass. It was covered with bayberries and sand roses. It was not an enemy—not a raccoon nor a hawk nor a fox. It was not a man; and yet, there was something about it that frightened him. Then it got up and moved. It settled down and was still, the wind twisting the branches that adorned it. For ten more minutes the birds circled their nest. Finally Larus dropped to the earth and his mate followed him. He went to the nest and sat down. He forgot the strange dome.

His mate stood beside him preening. Larus's eyes became starey. This was her signal to go. She lifted off the ground and winged east across Sachem Pond to Grove Point Rock. She alighted and scanned the sea for the bright-finned skipjacks that swam there. The surface of a wave twinkled with silver fins, She skimmed out, alighted, and stabbed them.

The morning was now bright. Over the gullery sea gulls circled softly. Others went down to the beach near the lab to preen. A few chased sand crabs. Others drifted off to Old Harbor for it was time for the fishing boats to come in and discard cleanings from the fish.

Larus sat serenely. Suddenly he flattened his feathers and stood up, wings drooped. The burlap dome was moving toward the gullery.

"Hahaha-hahahaha" Larus called. He spanked the air to rise. The dome moved toward a gull nest, paused, and went down the sand bank to the beach. Larus circled it, sensing a new threat to his nest and his mate and his egg. He grew terribly excited. He called the alarm cry of the gulls until birds from the Bay of Cows flew to see what was the matter.

The dome resting on the beach did not say

"enemy" to any of the other gulls. They could not call "Hahaha-hahahaha" because nothing caused the same reaction Larus had to the dome. But Larus did not give up. He braced his wings against a moderate wind and hung there.

Then Dr. Rivers stepped out of the dome with his notepad and camera. Larus dropped like a stone and struck the man across the back. The alarm he cried out brought the bird's friends, the wives, bachelors, and a group of gulls loafing on the ocean. He even summoned his rivals, the Yanks. They were united when they faced outside threats.

Dr. Rivers stepped back into the dome, and shouldering it, slowly made his way down the beach toward home. Larus was no longer inspired to anger when the burlap dome passed the lighthouse. His feelings were most intense at his nest. They grew feebler as he flew away from the club, and almost exactly at the lighthouse he stopped feeling altogether. These were his territorial emotions. He had others. He could be afraid anywhere of hawks, foxes, dogs, snakes, people, and particularly Dr. Rivers.

By now it was eight o'clock. Luke had overslept. He awoke to hear his father hammering in the lab below. Chinquapin was singing in her loft room next to his, as she dressed to go to work. Only a board wall separated them so he had to listen to all the words of her song. For a moment Luke lay trying to fight down the resentment of the night before. Then slowly he dressed and climbed down the ladder to the lab. His father was working on a box with springs and wires. Luke ran his fingers through his hair and tried to say brightly, "Another test?" But it came out flat.

Dr. Rivers looked up and grinned at his son. "Yep. We've completed the tapping tests. I'm sending the data off to Columbus to have it computed in the IBM machines. We're coming out where Tinbergen did." He leaned over a chart. "The baby gulls *do* react to the color red first and foremost—then to the lollipop shape. All of which proves that herring gulls react to specific things in their world—specific colors and shapes. I doubt if a mother is any more to a new chick than a lollipop with a red mark on it."

"I'm starved," Chinquapin called to her mother who was washing her face in a basin of cold water.

"Fix some bacon for us all," she said. "Working girls still have to help about the house."

"Pooh," she answered, but went off to do as she was told.

Luke looked over his father's shoulder. "Now what?" he said, gesturing toward the contraption.

"I want to try the tests the other way around now. I want to see what the parents react to. It could be that it's just the tapping and not the little chick at all. Could be it's the chick. Or maybe it's the down and fuzz plus the tap. Anyway, I'm building three boxes. We'll put the gulls in here," he pointed to the front of the first box, "and this smooth, shapeless object will just tap them. This will be Box A."

Despite himself Luke began to warm to the project.

"Box B will be a stuffed chick with its mouth open, rigged up to tap. And Box C will be a shapeless fuzzy thing that taps."

Chinquapin burst into the lab.

"Your bacon's ready. I'm off to work." Her smile was a sparkle.

Luke waited silently until the door closed behind her. "What do you want me to do today?" he asked dispiritedly.

"See if Larus and his mate have laid another egg. We ought to wind up those egg studies this week. Don't take this clutch away from them, but you might add an egg to 472. They've got three again. I was out this morning photographing them."

"Okay, but I think it's silly to go on. Fourteen out of fourteen gulls have laid three eggs and stopped whether we take eggs or add eggs. Seems to me we've proved they lay three, no more no less. Just because your song sparrow kept on laying egg after egg when you removed one doesn't mean the gulls ever will." Luke stomped to the kitchen, but called back, "But . . . you're the boss. If you need more data I'll try to get it."

"I do," replied his father firmly.

At noon Luke returned and reported the new egg in Larus's nest.

"And I put one of the square eggs in 472's nest," he said. "They're incubating all four as if nothing were wrong." He glanced at the nearly completed boxes. "And Orange-Blue's eggs have been destroyed . . . raccoons, I think. They're sucked and licked clean as a whistle. I saw them both out hunting yesterday and wondered what was up."

"Did you make notes of all that?"

"Of course I did!" Luke's voice showed his irritation.

"I think you ought to put another egg in Larus's nest."

"Oh, come on, those poor birds. Can't we let them alone?"

"It bothers you, not them." Luke turned toward the window. His heart sank as he watched Captain Gregory's green lobster boat move out to sea, the water shining around it like a sheet of silver. At the beach, sandpipers were running in the foam at the edge of the water.

"I can't get the shakes out of Box C," he heard his father say. He turned to look. When his father pushed the treadle on the outside, the fuzzy object arose with a wobble.

"I'll just have to make a note of it and discount the error in the results," he said. "I can't fix it."

The boat on the horizon was still on Luke's mind. "Why do we have to study dickey birds!" he suddenly blurted. "Why couldn't you go into physics? People care about physics. Who cares what we're doing out here . . . birds . . . everyone thinks we're queer."

His father looked up from the boxes with a startled expression; then he said with a frown, "Look, Luke, pure research is pure research, whether it's physics or bird behavior. I do it because I love to inquire into nature."

"But how about us? We always have to worry about the budget, and give up this and forget that because things are too expensive . . . I don't think we ask for much, Dad. A few gay clothes, a pair of red shoes . . . a trip West that I would have paid for myself."

"Luke!" his father's voice barked. "A man can only do what he must, even if it seems to hurt those he loves. If I'm honest with myself you'll learn to be honest with yourself. As far as I'm concerned there's nothing more to living than knowing what you are, whether you're a physicist, a dickey-bird man, or a waiter in a hotel."

"I know, I know. I've heard that all my life." Luke tried to hold back his anger.

"This is hard, lonely work for a boy. I know that. I would like to be as needed as a physicist is. But things change. Yesterday biologists were the important men . . . today the world needs physicists . . . tomorrow it may be beachcombers. But you can't go on the whims of society. You have to follow yourself. And to me, knowledge, any knowledge—even why birds react as they do—is a contribution to the mystery of life."

Luke felt miserable, as he always did when there was friction between himself and his father. He knew he should not shout and get angry, but the anger was there. He didn't know why. It seemed he just had to fight this man he loved.

He went to the kitchen to get some lunch. I guess I'm like the gull chicks, he thought. They have to peck because they see a red spot. I have to peck because something else is there. And, as he thought this, his anger died. He was surprised to feel it go. "Maybe there is something to dickey-bird knowledge," he said to his mother.

She looked at him strangely. "Stop talking to yourself and eat."

Luke went to Rebel Hill in the afternoon dressed in his black rubber coat and pith helmet and made notes on the number of times the chicks were fed. The very new ones were fed every twenty-five minutes.

Around four o'clock a thunderstorm gathered to the southwest and boomed over the island. Luke stood up, stretched, and glanced out at the ocean, worried about Chinquapin on a hostile sea. He wondered if it would be a good idea to take the boat out and find her. Suddenly out of a dark sky a flash of lightning ripped. It was immediately followed by an explosion of thunder. The thunder rolled around Rebel Hill. A wing flap caught Luke's eye. He lifted his binoculars and saw the five-day-old Spacecraft flop and lie stiff. Its wings were on the ground, its eyes wide, its neck was pulled in. Luke frowned as he quickly wrote down the time and the date and what he had seen. Then, walking slowly down the dune, he wondered again what was the matter with the little gull, and guiltily remembered how he had dropped the bird just after it was born.

Rain was falling. One by one the gulls left their loafing spots and flew back to the dunes to cover their young. Luke decided it would be foolish to search for the lobster boat. He sat down on the beach and listened to the rain strike the sand.

"Hahaha-hahahaha."

Luke glanced up to see Larus soaring home. He sailed overhead, beating his way against a bumpy wind. Fanning, dancing wing-flashes marked the great bird's descent to his nest.

Over the beach spanked the swift feet of Chinquapin. "Luke! Luke!" she called.

He jumped up in relief and ran to meet her.

Her face was glowing, and her words tumbled over each other, "We caught fourteen whoppers today. One weighed eleven pounds . . . his claws were as big as my head . . . and . . ." she stopped, out of breath with running and excitement.

"That's nice." he said, and wondered why he had worried about her.

The storm blew inland. Finally the rain stopped, but the dark clouds and twilight lowered the light early. Half an hour before their usual bedtime, the gulls got up on their wings and circled their breeding grounds. Luke watched them from the doorway of the lab. One by one they dropped below the horizon of humped sand dunes. They're like dancers running offstage, he thought. The night is their curtain. He watched them rise and fall, rise and fall until the final curtain of darkness fell and the last bird was still.

The Three Boxes

Two days later, on June the twelfth, Luke's father had completed plans for the new test. Dr. Rivers decided they would change their schedules and work at night. Darkness would give them an advantage; they could slip up on the sleeping birds and capture them without disturbing them too much.

Dr. Rivers and Luke sat at the table working out the details of the plan. The test-bird would be gently wrapped in a black cloth to keep it from beating and breaking its wings. "And we've got to come up with some disguise," his father said, "so we don't wake up the whole gullery and send them thrashing into the dark. My burlap dome decorated with shrubbery is beginning to make them suspicious."

Luke thought a moment. "What about soaking an old blanket in glue and then dipping it in sand? We could put that over us, lie on our bellies, and inch up on them. We'd look like a sand pile."

"Hmmm, maybe," replied his father. "Well, we could try it. I nominate you 'Specialist in Charge of Disguise.' "

Luke worked most of the next day on his plan. By late afternoon he finally got the right mixture of turpentine, varnish, and sand applied to an old army blanket. His father was pleased with Luke's creation and anxious to get on with the experiment. He suggested they get to bed right after supper so they could get up at midnight and begin.

So at seven-thirty that night, with the test boxes, the 3 by 5 cards and the nesting maps ready, they fell asleep. Luke was a little resentful at having his entire existence so completely rearranged, but when the alarm went off at midnight, he sat up in bed and realized he was excited. He had thought up the sand rug. Now it would be fun to see how it worked.

The first bird Luke captured bit him on the hand so hard he bled. Ruefully, he remembered his father's hard lesson when he netted Larus the first time. He carried the bird back, and the next time he used rubber bands to snap around the strong fierce beaks. But he was raked by the bird's big middle toe nail, so the third time out he carried a sock to put on the bird's feet. After that, Luke and his father worked quietly and carefully until dawn. Five birds had been tested.

"Pretty good," his father said.

Then his father cleared off the lab table and began to study the results. His enthusiasm was as high as it had been five hours earlier. "This is odd," he said, "Box C, with the shapeless fuzzy thing that taps—the one that wobbles—gets the most response. I didn't expect that! If it's the fuzziness plus the tapping that causes response, why doesn't Box B, which looks like a chick, get more response than Box C? Maybe it's a matter of the gull's-eye-view again."

Luke was too tired to care. He crawled slowly up his ladder while his father was still talking. A light shone through the cracks in his wall, meaning that Chinquapin was up. He knocked on the small door between their lofts. "Come in," she whispered. She was sitting cross-legged on her cot, writing in a book.

"Oh, Luke!" she bubbled, still in a whisper. "I've got $36 now! Isn't that wonderful?"

Luke couldn't deny that it was. He tried to swallow his envy, and replied gamely, "It sure is." Then, looking at her cheerful face, he broke out "Darn! I wish I could work. Why can't you help Dad now, and give me a week on the boat? It would be a good change for you. Isn't it heavy work?"

"It is," she confessed. "But I don't care. I want enough money to buy records and pay for pickles and cokes at the Hive next year. Besides, I can't catch a gull." She grinned.

Luke grinned back, amused at her sudden pride in that particular failure. He sat on the end of her cot and mused, "Now that we're working nights, maybe I could get a job. During the day I could wait on tables at one of the hotels."

"But Luke, you're so good!" Chinquapin exclaimed seriously. "Why should you work? You're so good at special things. You could win a scholarship . . . I'll bet the National Science Foundation would give you tons of money for just one of your science ideas."

Luke looked at her gratefully. There *were* things he could do. He knew he could. "Well, maybe. . . ." he said with an embarrassed shrug. He got up, said "Night," and returned quietly to his room. He stretched out on his cot and stared at the ceiling. Maybe he could write for *The Wilson Bulletin,* the bird journal. He could write about a day with Larus —they liked articles like that. Then he remembered. They didn't pay. People wrote for the Bulletin for love and prestige.

He rolled onto his side. He was good at science.

He could be a lab assistant. But where? Block Island was the end of the earth.

Suddenly Chinquapin's words came back. Why didn't he apply for a grant? He sat up. But what? What could he do? The National Science Foundation had funds for outstanding high school students. But you had to send them an outline for research. I'll think of something tomorrow, he said to himself, and punched his pillow into shape.

He was up before his father. The sun was high in a brilliant sky, the ocean was rocking gently. He put on his bathing trunks and ran to the beach feeling confident and strong. He was going to get a scholarship, maybe four or five hundred dollars, and then he could be on his own.

It was just a matter of thinking up a study. He trotted up the beach to the point. Running feels good, he thought, as his muscles stretched and worked. The air filled his lungs. He had to get in shape! It was this sitting around that made him so unhappy. He needed a workout every day. A man's body was his spirit . . . he ought to take care of it . . . a mile run up and down the beach would be good and then a hard swim to the rocks.

He sprinted across the sand, head back, fists tight, and hit the sea with his chest. He took a deep breath and went under. As he opened his eyes beneath the water he saw the green kelp float by. The sargassum weed with its air pockets tossed on the surface. Luke came up for air and stroked rhythmically into the Atlantic.

As he swam, the color of the water changed from the blue at the edge of the sea to a sudden dark brown. He knew he was in a plankton bed, the vital food basket of the ocean. Everything from oyster babies to the great whales feeds on it. Luke slowed down to look at the plankton, took some water in his mouth, rolled over on his back, and blew it into the sky. He smacked his lips and treaded water. He took another mouthful of sea water, because it seemed to him it was not very salty. In fact, the water was almost saltless. He wondered about it. I'll bet plankton filters the salt out of the sea, he thought.

After one more taste he forgot the whole thing, spun over, and swam to the rocks. Catching his breath he returned to Sandy Point, and rode the waves into shore. The last wave beached him high. As it trickled away he sat up, and heard Larus the sea gull call "Hahaha-hahahaha."

He ignored the bird. He stretched out and dozed in the sun.

For the next week life followed a similar pattern. Luke and his father worked from midnight to dawn.

The number of tested birds grew and grew, much to Dr. Rivers's pleasure—and to his distress, Box C, with the fuzzy thing that tapped but did not even look like a chick, and wobbled besides, kept getting the strongest reactions. The birds began to choke up baby food the second time the treadle tapped them. What caused it; what caused it?

They continued to test. On Saturday night, when Chinquapin was at the movies with Ginny, Luke sat on his cot, wrapped his hard brown arms around his knees, and listened to the night. This was the first time he had really relaxed in a week, and again his thoughts turned to his plans to get a grant. The tide was high, and he could hear the waves breaking close to the lab.

What would he do for that fellowship? The sound of the waves lapped on his memory. He remembered his swim into the brown plankton and how the water tasted fresh. Suddenly he had it! Everyone was interested in getting fresh water from the sea. He was certain that the plankton diluted the salt of the ocean. All he had to do was prove it. Perhaps the small plants and animals of the plankton took the salt into their cells. He could find how they did it and purify sea water with plankton. What an idea! His thoughts were coming so fast, and Luke was so excited he stumbled over the foot of his cot as he searched for paper.

Sometime later he heard Chinquapin return from the movies. As she climbed her steps from the kitchen and slipped into bed, Luke was just finishing the outline of his project to the National Science Foundation. During the next hour he recopied it. Then he wrote an accompanying letter and put them both in an envelope. His hand shook as he sealed it. He placed it on his clothes chest. Tomorrow he would meet the Point Judith ferryboat and mail it.

Hardly an hour later the alarm went off and he got up to work on the gullery. The results were consistent. As the sun came over the sea and sand, Luke's father was again trying to make meaning of the tap. Counting, comparing the time of night, the temperature, and the age of the bird, Dr. Rivers was crouched over his data as Luke went up his ladder.

He paused at the top and looked pityingly down on his father counting gull taps. He thought of Chinquapin stringing stinking fish together. His project made these look so petty. Even the boys that had gone West on the trip would be impressed. Wait until he told them how plankton made fresh water in the sea!

The next noon, Luke started off for Old Harbor with the letter in his pocket and his notebook on his belt. He might as well get notes for his father until he heard about his scholarship. He stopped and anchored in the Bay of Cows and timed a group of gulls loafing on the broad beach. When the tide turned, they beat their wings, and in twos and twenties, went out to sea. Luke followed them. He saw that the skipjacks were running, and realized that the gulls had definite reasons for loafing where they did. They knew two things: that the tide was changing and that it brought little fish to the surface.

Luke glanced up from his notebook to see the ferryboat come slowly over the horizon. He started the motor and sped toward Old Harbor, noting as he went, the bands on the gulls that were flying out to meet the ferry. The boat, he thought, seemed brighter than any ferry he had ever seen.

When he reached the dock, he saw that Larus, the magnificent gull, was on the pole of Captain Gregory's shack. He was staring at his feet. Luke started to write this down, but his mind was not on it. He could think of nothing but getting his letter on the ferryboat. To kill the last few minutes before it docked, he walked to the spring house to talk to Abnormality. He and Polly were resting in the shade just inside the house.

"Hi, Abnor!"

"Luke!" he smiled. "Pleased. Pleased. I am so pleased. Come on in."

It was not clean inside so Luke sat down against the door frame. He lifted his binoculars and focused on the boat. Polly grunted and went to sleep.

Abnormality was sorting the treasures he had picked up on the beach that morning. Luke watched the ferryboat grow bigger and bigger. He waited until its bow entered the stones of the breakwater, then jumped to his feet to meet it.

As soon as the gangplank touched the splintered wood of the dock, Luke pushed through the crowds of summer visitors and ran to the mailbox in the cabin. He dropped his letter and listened to it fall. Then he waved vigorously to the captain and light-footed it between bikes and dogs, fishermen and sunburned women toward the lobster shack.

The lobster boat was in and Chinquapin and Ginny were stringing fish. As Luke came toward the door he could see that they had guests—Hank Brown and Nat Mika, the two boys who worked in the Sea Food Restaurant across the harbor. The boys were sitting on barrels talking to the girls. Hank rose and shoved Chinquapin's shoulder affectionately. Luke was instantly annoyed. He did not like the inference of the shove, and he didn't like the idea of a tough kid like Hank hanging around his sister. Chinquapin had never had to deal with such people, and Luke didn't want her to have to learn now.

Chinquapin cried, "Stop that." She leaned over the stinking barrel and tried to go on stringing fish. "I can't work with you around," she said in an uneven voice.

Luke broke into a run as he saw Hank grin and come closer to her. "Aw, baby, you're cute when you're mad," he said. He took her chin in his hand. Chinquapin tried to push him away but both hands were full of fish. Tears of indignation filled her eyes. "Keep your hands off her!" Luke shouted as he bolted through the doorway.

Hank let go of Chinquapin's chin and spun around. "Well, well, here's big brother," he sneered, but he stuck his hands in his pocket and shrugged. Nat snickered.

Luke was smothering with fury. "Get out, both of you, and quick!" he yelled.

"Yeah, says who?" demanded Hank.

Nat came up behind him and said in a mimicking voice, "Yeah, says who?"

"I say so, and you'd better get packing," answered Luke. He was mad enough to knock their heads together, in spite of the fact that they were each almost as big as he was.

"All right, that's enough!" a deep voice boomed from behind them. It was Captain Gregory. He strode into the lobster shack and grabbed both Hank and Nat by the collar. "Get out, you two, and stay out!" he roared as he propelled them out the door.

The two boys wriggled under the iron grip of the Captain, and as they passed by Luke, Hank glared at him with outraged defiance.

"They won't be back," the Captain said reassuringly to the girls.

But Luke had the feeling that this would not be the end of the matter. He turned and left the lobster shack, troubled by this new aspect of Chinquapin's working for Captain Gregory. He couldn't stand the thought of her being exposed to rough characters like this, and yet he couldn't say anything about it to his father. Chinquapin had made such an issue over taking this job that Luke knew she herself would not complain, or even mention the incident. And if he brought it up, it would sound like sour grapes.

He went back to the motor boat and circled the island slowly. On the eastern side he found fifty gulls loafing and preening. He carefully read the color bands and put them down in his notebook. It was not easy but he wanted to take precise notes, now that his letter was on its way. He would soon be on a project that mattered—getting fresh water from the sea. It would be wonderful to be applying his scientific skills to a practical idea that would help people. No more of this pure research his father kept harping on.

A bird came over the island and pulled in on its left wing. It dropped, caught itself, dropped, and finally alighted on a big seaweed-covered rock. Luke saw that it was Orange-Blue. He wrote this down, propped his elbows on his knees, and waited for the bird to do something. Fifteen minutes passed, and the bird was still in the same position. Luke's arms began to ache. This was the most difficult part of science—the long intervals when nothing happened. He wondered if his plankton study would be like this, but he put the thought out of his mind and went on watching the gull.

He got back to the lab just as Chinquapin came over the dune from work. She ran past Luke without thanking him or even mentioning the incident that afternoon. He watched her open the lab door and rush to hug her father.

Luke smiled and kicked the sand. The little chick sees the nest and the parent and is motivated to run very fast to safety. And he felt very superior.

The Wobble

Luke was on his belly under his sand blanket at dawn, ready to capture one last bird for testing that night. He was close to Spacecraft's nest and watched him fondly for a minute. The bird was big now, nineteen days old, but still unable to fly. Occasionally he practiced by standing on his nest, flapping his wings, but he could not get off the ground. The gift of flight does not come easily to the sea gull.

The sand blanket jerked and Spacecraft opened his gray and black eyes. He blinked in the twilight of·morning, his eyes wide, his feathers flat. Just then a night jet from the Navy burst across the sky.

Spacecraft pulled in his neck and froze. His eyes had widened, and he did not move for several minutes. Then he fell into a crouch.

I'm beginning to think Spacecraft is conditioned to crumble when he hears thunder or a jet, Luke thought. He lifted the bird from its roost and wrapped it in sheeting, put a rubber band on its beak, and wiggled down the dune. He handed the bird to his father when he got back to the lab, and took out his notebook. Under Spacecraft he noted, "June 23, 4:02 A.M. Spacecraft terribly afraid. Jet went over."

He had been taught not to write down his opinion so he did not add the obvious correlation that the sound of the jet might have had something to do with Spacecraft's behavior. It had become second nature for Luke to follow his father's advice. He knew it took many, many objective notes to find the truth. Opinions would not do. Luke felt very scientific as he wrote down other things he had observed. One of them might be the unexpected answer to Spacecraft's strange actions when he went over all the cards later. "Pale light, cool, mother standing outside nest. Spacecraft did not see me. I was well hidden under blanket." He had better keep in training for his plankton project.

Luke heard his father begin the test, humming to himself in satisfaction. Dr. Rivers happily placed the adult bird in the first box. Luke heard the taps of the A machine with its smooth shape, then the B machine with its dummy chick, and finally C with its fuzzy shape that wobbled.

"Same thing. Box C makes the old bird fairly cluck and coo."

Luke had lost interest. His mind was full of his own wonderful idea and he couldn't be bothered about the taps of gulls. He walked toward the door and stretched, looking off into the dawn.

"I'm tired," he said.

His father ignored him. "Look at this. It drives me in circles. We're sitting on top of something very exciting and I can't see it."

He sat back and ruffled his hand through his hair. frowning in perplexity. "I've got to think a new way. I need a man from Mars with a wholly different point of view to see through this data. Evidently the essence of a baby gull isn't a fuzzy gull chick, nor is it a tapping gull chick. The parent gull feels one more thing. Something in Box C!"

Luke's mother came out of the bedroom, looking sleepy. "You two! Aren't you ever going to bed?" She wrapped her terry cloth robe tighter and stretched.

"Do gulls ever yawn?" she asked.

Luke stared at his father. For all their gull studies, neither could answer her.

"There's too much to know, Marge," replied Dr.

Rivers. "Life, even a sea gull's life, is mysterious. Come here and look at this. The box that looks the least like a chick gets the most response. What do you suppose we're doing wrong?"

Luke's mother peered in the boxes and pushed the treadles. Then she straightened up and said with a twinkle, "You men have absolutely no paternal feelings. The thing in Box C has jerky movements. It wobbles like an infant—any infant, human or gull. It looks so helpless. Of course the birds feel parental. Why, the funny little movements of a baby make you want to soothe it and take care of it. Anyone knows that!"

Luke looked aghast at his mother. She had in one minute answered the question they had spent days trying to answer.

"Marge! Oh Marge, you're right!" cried Dr. Rivers. "It's exactly what the data are shouting at me. A tiny kitten has a wobbly head, a robin shakes and jerks as it reaches up for food, calves wobble, puppies tremble, and infants jerk. Luke, we've got it. Parent gulls respond strongly to awkwardness—especially if it taps." He hurried to his bookshelf and thumbed through the flimsily bound magazines that were studies on young monkeys and geese.

Luke went to the sheets of notes and studied them. How clear it all seemed. His heart sank a little as he thought of finding the secret of the plankton. It might take longer than he thought. Would he have the ability to set up the proper tests, and then be able to apply the right insight? He touched the stack of notes and papers prepared by his father and wondered for the first time how he would begin his investigation. He really had no idea. The thought made him tired. He picked up the bird and quietly returned it to the gullery.

The gulls awakened soon after Luke fell asleep. They winged softly on the thermal currents to the beaches for crabs, and out over the ocean for fish. The juveniles like Spacecraft stayed home and flapped their wings unattended by either parent. Each stayed in his own territory. That was a law of the gullery and one of the first things the young herring gulls were taught. Death awaited the bird that didn't learn this.

A few hours later Luke was awakened by gull commotion. They were crying as if a million foxes had descended upon their gullery. "What's going on?" he wondered and crouched at his low window. Frantic gulls dived and circled the sandspit.

"Hahaha-hahahaha" Larus screamed and winged to attack.

What on earth was out there? Luke wondered, as he watched the birds dive and choke up. He looked for an enemy of the gulls somewhere in the bright sun and sand. Then he saw his father dashing for the water. Luke laughed.

They do hate him, he thought. The poor man can't even put a toe out the door but what they crash down upon him. I guess he's netted and banded and captured so many, he's become more frightening than an eagle. Luke peered into the shining sun and water. Conditioning is an interesting thing, he mused, and it's very real. Take those mad birds above Dad's head. They're conditioned to fear him, and their fears make them behave in a certain manner: they dive and throw up food.

On the glittering horizon Luke saw the flat squat shape of the ferryboat. He was tempted to go and meet it, but he knew it was too soon to receive an answer to his letter. In fact, he thought, the letter is just getting to Washington. He saw the secretary open it. She read it with excitement, then hurried to the chairman of the scholarships and thrust it at him. Luke could see him reading it. Then the chairman rose in astonishment and called his assistant. Presently, three Ph.D's gathered to read the letter. Their excitement was high. They sat down at a large walnut table and argued whether to give Luke Rivers $500 or $1000. One man said the idea was so revolutionary he ought to get $1500, but they didn't have that much money.

Luke grinned as he saw himself with the check.

He put it in the bank and got a checkbook. He ordered books. That seemed the way to begin. Then he imagined himself at the college clothes store. He bought a dark suit, a top coat, new belts and shirts. In his new suit he threw back his shoulders and tightened his back muscles. He looked at himself in the mirror. The image was conservative but expensive. Luke approved. A top-notch scientist should look just this way; neat, thoughtful, collected. His parents had always insisted that clothes didn't matter, that the world took a man at his own evaluation of himself. But Luke never had made much sense out of this family wisdom, for it seemed to him that if a man evaluated himself highly he would certainly put good clothes on his back.

Suddenly Luke snapped out of his reverie. The gulls had stopped "hahaing" and were calling soft mew calls. He knew his father had come indoors, because the birds were saying, "The enemy is gone, and all is well with the world." He swung down the ladder to the lab. His father had just returned.

Luke sorted out the field cards for the day, then picked up his binoculars and told his father he wanted to follow Larus for a few hours. This kind of tedious discipline would be needed in the months to come, he thought. His father thought that was a good plan, as he was computing the box data and wanted to be alone.

Larus was on his nest. The bird was sitting low, gazing at nothing, for it was the fifteenth day of incubation for this clutch of eggs, eleven more to go. Luke wrote down, "Incubating; 2:30," then observed three juveniles. They were as large as Spacecraft, and still awkward and clumsy. He was amused to see one run up and down the grass corridors on its territory. It would stop at the edge of its land and peer into the next territory like a curious child. Immediately the mother bird on the next nest would flatten her feathers and stretch her neck, like a schoolteacher snapping her fingers at a prank-minded boy. The young gull ran away from the stretched neck, went to another border, and repeated the same thing.

It makes you understand where some feelings come from, Luke said to himself. Like wanting to chase people off your land, or being scared when a big person threatens you. He shook his head in wonder and lifted his glasses again.

Luke studied Larus for the rest of the afternoon. He was a little annoyed to discover he was developing an affection for that bird because he wouldn't be studying gulls much longer. To develop such a feeling now was almost a waste of time.

Defense
of Territory

The following day Luke was in the lab alone. His father and mother had driven to the store. He thumbed through his father's neatly arranged monographs and books until he came to plankton. Then he sat down and read. Thousands and thousands of plants and animals made up the great mass of life. Each had a long name and most were too small to see without a microscope. Completely absorbed, Luke did not bother to move when the back door opened and Chinquapin and Ginny came in. He read on, vaguely hearing the conversation in the kitchen, but paying no attention.

"Where's everybody?" Ginny asked.

"I dunno," Chinquapin answered. The food cabinet swished open and there was the plunk, plunk, plunk of food being set out. Chairs scraped as the two girls settled themselves at the table. The wind blew and thumped against the house, the sea beat the sand. Chinquapin said she was tired, and she talked about the long day. It had begun at 5:00 A.M. when she got up and biked to Old Harbor. They had sailed at six and arrived at Captain Gregory's lobster area around seven. The pots had been full and heavy, the sea tossing and rough. She spoke ruefully of three bandages on her hands that marked brief but painful encounters with lobster claws. She was glad the day's work was done.

The conversation changed, and Ginny said, "It's eerie out here with only the noises of the wind and the gulls."

"When I was little I used to like it," said Chinquapin, "But now it's just a bore." There was a pause with only the birds crying softly over the dunes. They sounded lonely and plaintive. Then Chinquapin said briskly, "The heck with gulls. I want people, lots and lots of people, and things happening and noise and laughter!"

Ginny's voice was still subdued.

"I don't understand what your father does with the birds," she said. "I mean . . . he doesn't sell them, or anything . . . does he really just look at them?"

Chinquapin made an impatient sound, and then a note of pride came into her voice.

"The difference is this," she said carefully. "Some people sell things, some people study things."

"But what good does it do to study a gull?"

"What do you mean, 'good'?"

"I mean, who cares what a gull does?"

"Some day it might be important—and anyway it's Dad's job," Chinquapin said in exasperation.

Luke lifted his head as the tail end of their conversation penetrated his consciousness, then with a wry smile, he delved back into his books.

Ginny had stopped talking. The girls ate in silence as the waves rode heavily up the beach and collapsed. The gulls mewed and winged overhead.

Suddenly, in the midst of the quiet world of the sea and gulls, there was a knock at the door.

After a small silence, Chinquapin said in a stunned voice, "Oh—Hank and Nat!"

"Hi, there!" said Nat. "How's tricks, Baby?"

"Just thought we'd pay a sociable call, drop in and have some tea," added Hank. Both boys guffawed loudly.

Chinquapin's voice rose to a high pitch.

"Go on home," she said, "Nobody's here. We're busy."

The screen door squeaked as it opened and banged shut.

There was a scuffling sound of feet and chairs.

"Nat, we're not kidding. Go away!" Ginny snapped.

"Aw, let's dance," cried Hank. There was more scuffling, and then Chinquapin said in a terrified voice, "Let me go!"

Suddenly Luke snapped to. It dawned on him what he was hearing in the background was not a dream but was actually happening. He made it to the door in two leaps, and thundered, "Get out!"

Chinquapin saw Luke in the doorway, and closed her eyes in relief.

Luke took one look at the two boys who were slicked up but still rough and scruffy, and his instinct was to knock the stuffing out of them this time. But his common sense stopped him. He could not take on two; he would be beaten up. He thought hard, and then the perfect plan flashed across his mind.

"Birdie boy!" Hank shouted. He stopped teasing Chinquapin and swaggered toward Luke. "Well, now, here's our big tough pal."

"Aw, let's be friends," Luke said and extended his hand. "No hard feelings."

Taken off guard, Hank shook hands suspiciously.

Luke slapped him on the back. "Come on into the lab and take a look around. It's the greatest." He led the way toward the lab. Hank and Nat followed.

"You like birds?" Luke asked. "I'll show you some terrific birds." He reached for the pith helmet and slapped it on his head. "I wear hats in the sun."

Hank and Nat folded their arms and stood together like an armed fortress. They looked at Luke as if he were slightly loony.

"This is a bird lab, huh?" They roared with laughter.

"Whatta ya do to the little birdies? Tickle 'em?" The boys poked each other and laughed again.

Luke slipped into the raincoat. He put his arms around the boys and whispered. "Dontcha know what we do out here? Didncha ever hear?" They both stiffened.

"Come on, I'll show you the real stuff," Luke said, and steered them out the door toward the beach. He glanced back and saw Ginny and Chinquapin watching them in amazement.

"Wanna make an easy buck?" Luke went on. Nat looked from his friend's face to Luke's and back again. His eyebrows knitted. "Whoareya kiddin'?"

"Ever hear of cock fights?" Luke said. Nat nodded. Luke was leading them away from the lab toward the lighthouse. Hank drew back.

Luke talked fast. "Whatta ya think we do out here?

Dance with sea gulls? We fight 'em. Gull fights. Big business. You can clean up or lose a grand in one afternoon. They're fierce fighters. Fight to death!" Luke was beginning to enjoy himself. Now his audience was with him. He was thinking fast as he embroidered his story.

"Gull fights?" Hank said. "I never heard of 'em."

" 'Course not," Luke said in a low voice. "We keep it quiet. And no one can touch us out here in the Atlantic. We're beyond the three-mile limit." He was becoming positively inspired.

"Think all those fancy game boats that come to Old Harbor are for fishing? Huh? Don't be silly. They're cover-up for the real business . . . gull fights. Wanna see one?" Hank had stopped walking. He was turning things over in his mind.

"I always thought there was something more to this operation than met the eye," he said. "It figures . . . gull fights. . . ." His head nodded as it became clear to him.

"Yeah," Nat agreed. "Cheez, what a slick operation." He glanced back at the lab. The two girls were sitting in the sand, watching with wide grins on their faces.

Their expressions puzzled Nat for a moment. He hesitated. Quickly Luke put his arm around him, and swung him around.

"Got a buck? I'll make it five for you. I take care of

the birds. The fight tonight has odds of five to one, but the favorite is sick. He'll never make it . . . wanna bet on it?"

"Sure," said Hank.

Nat was not so easily taken. "Lemme see these gulls. Show me where they fight."

"Okay," Luke said. He led the way down the trail to Rebel Hill, talking fast about favorites and anything else he could remember from high school sports and the racing page of the local paper. He came up with another idea.

"You guys ever notice the bands on the gulls around here?"

"Yeah," Nat answered.

"Those are the males—the fighters—we mark 'em, so we can tell Sea Robin from Baby Grand." Birds were beginning to circle the boys and "hahahaing." Luke glanced up at them hopefully. Larus still had eggs. He could count on Larus. Orange-Blue was incubating, too.

"Where're the pens?" Nat asked suspiciously as they plodded up the shifting dune. "Dontcha pen 'em?"

"Why should we? They feed themselves. It's cheaper. They always come back. You see them over this dune every night dontcha?"

As they reached the edge of the nesting area, Luke

looked up and saw that his plan was working. Gulls dropped from the sky in great swirls.

The gulls attacked to defend their homes. Wings flashed and beat. Now the boys were in the midst of a raucous, furious cloud of gulls. Luke's helmet spun, but he felt wonderful. He laughed aloud at the glorious sight before him. The gulls were choking up all over Hank and Nat. The smell of putrid fish was everywhere. Luke held his nose, and watched as Hank turned green and Nat heaved and ran down the dune. The birds followed, striking, and choking up on the intruders.

A deed of love in the spring, of devotion to chicks in the summer, choking came easily to the gulls. Luke sat down and watched, marveling that somehow the birds knew their love token was offensive to everything but another gull.

He pushed away a crowd of birds around him and walked down the hill to see Nat and Hank plunge into the ocean. They paddled and swam toward Old Harbor.

Luke had one more inspiration. He called to the retreating figures, "And they'll get you next time, and the next, and the next. They never forget. So lay off!"

Covered with seafood, but pleased with himself, Luke ran back to the lab. He threw his hat and coat under the pump. Chinquapin and Ginny ran over to him.

"That was wonderful," Ginny said.

Chinquapin held tightly to his arm. "I want a husband just like you someday. You're great!"

And Defense
of Young

Luke and his father worked three more days on the tapping tests. Just before sunrise Luke took the last bird back to the gullery. The dawn was shining yellow over a dark sea. He stood still to watch the sun come up. Down on Rebel Hill, Spacecraft was flapping as he strengthened the muscles in his breast and wings. Then he rested with his wings open. Suddenly a gust from the hollow swept up the dune and lifted him off his feet. Spacecraft did not know he was launched until he glanced down and saw the beach grass passing under him.

The movement caught Luke's eye, and he lifted his binoculars to watch the flight of the young bird. Spacecraft was now drifting over another couple's territory. Luke held his breath—suppose Spacecraft should close his wings and fall to the ground? But, teetering and side-slipping, Spacecraft sailed down the hill and was dumped by the wind into the pit— the no man's land of gulls. Here he shook himself and looked around. He was obviously surprised and frightened. The laws of the gullery were deeply imprinted upon him, and now that he was off his land he knew that threats awaited him.

Spacecraft spread his wings and tried to jump on the air, and Luke saw that he was going to try to fly back. But then the bird stopped and stood still, and Luke realized that he had heard a signal. Out of the din of the awakening gullery a voice had checked him; the voice of his father. A moment later the big white gull stood beside his son. He choked up and fed him, then sat down beside him. Spacecraft also sat down. Luke watched to see how the parent would get the juvenile back to their own territory. The risk of flying was great since it was all uphill. But the birds only loafed, leaving Luke in suspense.

There was no point in waiting around; they might loaf for hours, as he well knew. Luke wandered back to the lab. His father was walking from the typewriter to the window to the library to the door. He was restless. Luke shrugged: his father had been this way ever since he had heard about the visit of Nat and Hank to the lab.

"I'm going to bed," Luke told him. "You'd better quit, too."

"Luke, what are the young people like at Old Harbor?"

"They're O.K., except for a few ruffians like Nat and Hank. Why?"

"I feel uneasy about Chinquapin working down there. She's pretty young."

Luke wanted to say something, but realized whatever he said would sound like, "I told you so." He just couldn't discuss Chinquapin with his father, and he was both resentful and chagrined. He turned in frustration and walked to the library. Plankton, he thought. Wait until I get that scholarship, then I can give Dad some money and he can tell Chinquapin to stop work. Why, I'll even give her some . . . no . . . I'll hire her to help. She could take care of the plankton.

He paused as his hand pulled a marine biology book from the case. He wondered how he would "take care" of plankton. Salt water aquariums were difficult to maintain but he couldn't keep dipping plankton out of the sea. Where would he get plankton in Ohio?

On his cot he tried to read but he could not concentrate. The book was technical, and furthermore the gulls were mewing over the lab. Each voice seemed to ask him, "How will Spacecraft get home?" It irritated him that he could not forget the gulls. He turned on his side and put the pillow over his ears. When he closed his eyes, he saw Spacecraft, wide-eyed and frightened, alone on the dune.

Luke could stand it no longer. He ran down the steps, threw on the raincoat and helmet, and hurried to Rebel Hill. Spacecraft and his father were not in the pit. Luke was disappointed. He ran down to where they had been. There he might see tracks on the sand that would tell him what had happened. But the footprints that were pressed on the fine top layer of wind-blown sand went around in circles. They seemed to go nowhere.

Before going up the hill to see if the birds were back on the nest, Luke dropped on his knees and looked through the beach grass. Perhaps Spacecraft and his father were hiding. He looked again. Up the entire dune side of Rebel Hill were corridors and tunnels, lacing in and out of each other to the top of the hill. Luke flattened on his stomach to study the labyrinths more closely. They obviously were made by sea gulls. What a discovery! How long had they been there?

A long hooked beak thrust out of a sunlit spot far down one corridor, then a head and eye appeared. A young gull peered at Luke. It pulled its head back when he moved. He tried to lie motionless. Several minutes went by. The beak appeared again, then the eye. Across the corridor another beak thrust out, and another eye. Luke tried not to laugh. Testily the young gulls walked into the green archways. It was too dark to read their bands but Luke could see what they were doing. One lifted its head slightly above another and dropped its wings. They sparred briefly, then ran up the hill. Luke jumped up to see where they were going and was just in time to see each go to his own territory.

This was evidently a place where the young gulls played together and imitated their parents, unharassed by the adults. It was off the nesting site, and therefore neutral ground. He lay down again and peered into the maze. The corridors led up the hill to the homelands of the parents. *That's* how Spacecraft got home, Luke almost said out loud, and hurried up the hill to see if his favorite bird was home. Indeed, Spacecraft was hunched beside his nest, sleeping off his morning adventure.

His spirits rose. Wait 'til I tell Dad about this. He'll be pleased for sure. And he plunged down the dune.

He burst into the lab, scarcely able to contain his elation. But his father had gone to bed. The lab was quiet; a stack of papers lay by the typewriter with

"End" penciled on the top sheet. Luke stared at it as the excitement trickled out of him. The word meant that the tapping study was done—after two long, hard weeks.

Suddenly the whole exhausting project swept over him again. The devil with juvenile birds, he said to himself, and climbed to his loft. In his dreams he saw the president of the National Science Foundation drinking the first glass of water from the sea. He smiled in his sleep.

Two days later Luke watched his mother type the last page of the tapping study. He and his father had just come from the gullery where they had been putting aluminum bands on the juvenile birds. Spacecraft's test flight had made the work urgent. The juvenile gulls they had not caught for the first tapping tests must be banded before they could fly.

As he chased them around their territory and down the corridors of grass Luke was amused. He whooped and hollered—and realized that the young birds had a society of their own. It would have been fun to study it, but he knew he should not start anything now. The scholarship would soon be announced and he would have to get to work on a real piece of research.

The next day moved along slowly. Luke's father

and mother proofread the article and got it ready to mail to the editor of a scientific journal. The weather was stormy. The clouds met the sea, and Block Island was lost in fog. Chinquapin had stayed home from work.

Breakfast was long since over when she came downstairs, so she carried a bowl of cereal into the lab to be with her family. As she sat at the table the bowl slipped. The milk splashed down her clean shirt.

"Oh, Christ!" she said and jumped up.

Luke stared at her.

The silence that followed seemed to echo around them.

"Chinquapin!" Dr. Rivers's voice boomed, "I'm done. You're not going back to work. My daughter will not use profanity."

Chinquapin was stunned herself, and frightened as she looked at her father. "I'm sorry," she said. "I won't do it again."

But it was as if she were not there. Luke watched his father gather up a batch of 3 by 5 lab cards, stack them, and put them away in a filing case. No one said a word. They just watched him.

Finally he said, "Marge, this ends the gull study."

"Ends what?"

"The gull study. I've been fooling myself. I thought this was a lovely way to spend our summers and raise children. But I see I'm mistaken. They need more. I'm going to Boston to get a job. Maybe the Audubon Society has something."

"Oh, Frank, now listen," she rallied. "Chinquapin is just trying her wings. I'm sure she won't talk that way anymore, will you, dear? Frank, you must finish your work. You really must!"

"No. I'm done. I see that this family has outgrown the gull study."

Luke watched his mother rise and put a hand on her husband's arm.

"Before you make up your mind, why don't you ask the Audubon Society if they have some scholarship funds? Maybe they could help us out."

Dr. Rivers paused, but his mouth was set grimly.

Chinquapin watched him, silently. Luke wished she would speak up, apologize, do something before their father got any more upset. But she only looked at him in fright. Or was it fright? Luke studied her small face closely. No, it was relief. She had been afraid. But now she was thankful that her father was making her quit her job. Luke realized she had stuck to it only because she had committed herself.

Into the crisis came the sound of the ferryboat. Luke jumped up. The scholarship! Maybe it had come. He would bike into the harbor and get the mail. Everything could be saved if only his grant were approved.

"Where are you going, Luke?" his father said sharply.

"To Old Harbor."

Dr. Rivers's voice was still tense. "While you're there, tell Abnormality to have the travel agency schedule his flight for June 30th, sometime in the afternoon. We're going to Boston. We'll give him a ride to Logan Airport."

"No!" thought Luke. He ran fast so that he would not hear his father saying "The gull study is ended," but the words seemed to bounce back from the sand no matter how hard he ran. He ran all the way to Old Harbor. He had not wanted to have to work on the gull study, and Chinquapin hadn't wanted to be restricted by it either, but neither of them had thought of their father. What would happen if he stopped working on it?

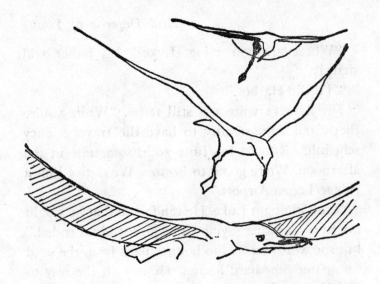

Abnormality

The letter was not there.

Two days later it still had not come, and Luke and his father met Abnormality at the dock, according to Dr. Rivers's schedule. Abnormality had shaved and his well-worn clothes looked clean. His empty blue eyes were bright in his bronze face as he grinned and waved at them. Luke drove up to the ferry slip in the beach wagon and waited while the boat unloaded cars and passengers from the mainland. Abnormality climbed into the front seat and waited with him.

As usual the summer tourists began to wind down the hill from the big hotel above the harbor to watch the boat, for the coming and going of the big ferry was the event of the day. Even Luke got caught up in the excitement. The captain leaned over the bridge and waved. Luke waved back. Sailors threw lines and clanged bells. Whistles tooted, and cars by the dozen rolled out of the vast hold of the boat. When it was empty, the cars on Block Island rolled forward to fill it.

A sailor signaled Luke up the gangplank into the clanging iron car port.

"You goin' somewhere, Abnor?" All the sailors on this run knew Block Island's favorite character.

"He's going to Chicago to see a psychiatrist," Luke explained as they climbed out of the car. Abnormality smiled cordially and walked toward a railing.

The sailor shook his head at Luke. "Nothing the matter with him. Any man that can have fun without working don't need no head-shrinker." They laughed together.

Luke followed Abnormality up the steps to the deck. They found Dr. Rivers on the far side of the boat staring over the rail into the sea. People began to fill the wooden seats along the deck. Suddenly Luke heard a shrill "Hahaha hahahaha." Larus dove out of the sky, slapped Dr. Rivers across the face with his wing, and swerved up to sit on the mast.

A nearby woman gasped and drew back. Three more gulls winged in, crying and diving. Their feathers sounded like taffeta in the wind. The woman was terrified, and Dr. Rivers escorted her gently into the cabin.

"I didn't know sea gulls attacked people," she said in a quavering voice.

Luke was proud of his father's courtliness. "Most of them don't. It's just a group on the tip of Block Island that would like to see a few of us who study them eradicated from this earth." He smiled and sat down, but the woman would have no more of him. She moved to the other side of the boat, away from the gulls and the man who attracted them.

An hour and a half later they debarked at Point Judith and in another hour they were within the limits of Boston. The old city spread low and misty along the bay. Luke leaned far out the window to smell and see this city of piers and masts and streets that wound without purpose. He was fond of Boston.

The airport was in sight of the bay, and the gulls drifting in the sun made him feel at home in the strange, busy world. But Abnormality was staring in fright at the world beyond Block Island. He crept out of the car and looked around him, whispering softly to himself.

"See any bands?" Dr. Rivers asked Luke as he peered at the gulls.

Luke lifted the glasses he had automatically worn around his neck, and focused on a wheeling bird that was mewing and side-slipping toward the bay. "Nope," he replied. "Not on this one."

"He's off to loaf," his father observed. "I couldn't mistake that flight. I wonder where they loaf in Boston?"

"At tea." Luke was pleased with himself for this sally. He smiled at Abnormality. Abnormality smiled back, but Luke knew he did not understand the quip. At least he seemed less nervous.

At the terminal Dr. Rivers checked Abnormality's ticket and reserved him a seat. Luke tried to talk to him in the confusion of the airport, but it was useless. Suddenly Abnor remembered something. He fumbled in his coat, found a piece of paper, and handed it to Dr. Rivers.

"Maybe you'd better call this famous doctor and tell him I'm coming." Luke's father looked at the name and assured Abnormality he would take care of it. He immediately put through a call to the psychiatrist in Chicago. He made plans with the doctor to have someone meet Abnor's plane. Dr. Rivers talked briefly and then hung up.

After Abnormality had gone up the ramp and the plane door had shut, Luke could not shake off his despondency.

"I think it's terrible to change him," he said as he walked with his father toward the big impersonal terminal.

His father put his hand on Luke's shoulder. "If he can be helped to be useful it would be better for him, wouldn't it?"

Luke wasn't so sure. "But I don't know anyone else who has a pet pig. We ought to have people with pet pigs. You know, he really believes that the sea and the beaches will take care of him so that he can heal people."

"I know."

"So what difference does it make? Why isn't his world all right? It works. And maybe he is useful, just by giving other people someone to smile over."

They stopped at the cyclone fence and looked back. It was just three o'clock—departure time.

The big silver bird taxied out into the sun, and hummed solidly down the runway, all jets firing smoothly. It moved slowly at first, then faster and faster. Screaming over the earth, it fired and thundered and gathered speed until it could do nothing else but fly. It rose shrilly and thrust straight up above the bay in the sunshine. As Luke squinted at it a cloud of herring gulls and starlings and terns sparked out around the plane like a sunburst.

Suddenly the shining jet tilted to the left. A chill went through Luke. He knew the plane would straighten out. It had to. But it did not. It dipped deeper to the left, hung motionless against the sky

like a great white cross, then slowly slipped earth-
ward. Down, down, down, faster and faster it dropped
until it hit the water. It screamed and went under.
A spout of steam shot up. It was rimmed with flame.
It, too, fell back into the bay, leaving the sky empty.

"No, God," Luke whispered. His father's hands
were digging into his arm. The airport was absolutely
silent.

Then the whirr of a siren arose. Motors started.
In one minute the whole airport was in action. Men
ran out doors, bells clanged, and from hangars and
garages, cars and trucks appeared.

Luke could see people dashing about like sand
crabs. Then they stood still, for now, rising slowly
out of the bay, came a cloud of smoke. It drifted into
the sky where it was carried by winds far out to sea.

"I guess that's all," Luke's father said finally. "I
guess there's nothing we can do."

"I guess not." They walked away from the fence.

They stood in the terminal building with other
stunned friends and relatives of the passengers on the
flight, feeling hollow and useless. Then a voice on the
public address system announced solemnly, "There
are no survivors on Airways Flight 9."

"Now what do we do?" Luke asked. It was a long
time since he had felt so young and helpless.

"I'll call Chicago. I know of nothing else to do."

Luke followed his father to the telephone. They waited in a hushed line for a long time, and finally the call went through.

Luke stood close to his father in the booth. He did not want to be alone.

"I'm sorry," he heard his father say. "You will tell his family, won't you? I don't know who they are. Perhaps you have their names."

Luke saw his father's shoulders sag. The circuit closed. "The psychiatrist was Abnor's brother," his father said quietly. "He's the only family there is."

Luke drove silently with his father to keep the appointment at the Audubon Society. Everything seemed very unreal, and when they were finally seated across the desk from the director, his father tried to speak with enthusiasm. He was telling of the Rebels and the Yanks and the tapping of the wobbly chicks. But Luke could see his father's heart was not in it.

Finally the director said, "If you were working on cardinals or bluebirds or some of the garden species that most of our people love, we could help you. In fact, I could give you a job right now teaching ornithology if you want it. Good pay. How about it?" When Dr. Rivers didn't respond, he added, "But nobody cares about sea gulls, really."

"I know," said Dr. Rivers. "I've felt that way ever

since three o'clock this afternoon. The study of sea gulls suddenly seems terribly useless and silly." He sighed heavily. "Thanks for the job offer. I may take it. But first I want to see if I can raise funds to at least finish this summer's work. I promised my wife I'd try."

He arose and shook hands. The director followed him to the door. "You know," he said, "you might go to Harvard. There's a zoologist there who is interested in research on behavior."

He scribbled a name on a card and handed it to Dr. Rivers. "Call him and tell him I said you ought to see him."

An hour later they arrived at the zoology department at Harvard. Dr. Born was grading summer school papers. Luke noted that he was obviously glad to meet his father, and he listened carefully to his story of the research on Block Island.

Then he said thoughtfully, "There are quite a few people around here interested in animal behavior, but they're all working with the Medical School. Unfortunately, I myself have no funds for behavior study. Let's go over to the Medical School and see if we can catch some of the key men before they leave for the night."

At the Medical School the scientists working late delayed their departures to listen to Dr. Rivers. They included Luke in the conversations, and he wondered as they talked whether these men might some day learn of his work on the plankton when he had completed his studies for the National Science Foundation.

When his father had finished explaining his project, one of the doctors said, "I could get you some funds if you weren't studying birds. There's a grant for research on monkeys, but none for birds. Monkeys are closer to humans." The other scientists nodded in agreement.

Dr. Rivers turned away. Luke could see that he was tired—very tired. And suddenly Luke himself wanted nothing more than to sleep a hundred years.

Weary as they were, neither wanted to spend the night in Boston. So they pushed on to Point Judith, where they spent the night in an old hotel by the sea so they could catch the first ferry in the morning. They hardly spoke all evening. There was nothing to say.

The Federal Aviation Agency

The people of Block Island stood quietly on the wharf as the early ferry brought Luke and his father home. Captain Gregory was towering above Ginny and Chinquapin. The postmaster, the game boat captains, the owner of the grocery store—all were there. Their faces were quiet, anxious.

Luke and Dr. Rivers walked down the gangplank and into the crowd. Dr. Rivers told the painful story of Abnormality.

"Do they know what went wrong with the jet?" Captain Gregory asked out of the silence.

"I haven't heard," Dr. Rivers answered, "and I didn't ask . . . it was all so red and white and . . . final."

The tide was out as they drove down the beach to the Sea Bird Lab. Huddled far out on the lonely spit, the gray structure looked warm and comforting. The birds that swung over it caught Luke's heart, and suddenly the numbness that had gripped him unlocked and he put his face in his hands and sobbed for Abnormality. His father softly gripped his knee.

As they neared the lab, they saw Mrs. Rivers running down the beach to meet them. "Did you see it?" she asked when they drew alongside her.

Luke's father nodded and closed his eyes. He climbed out of the car and said in a weary voice, "Marge, I've been kidding myself. This is the industrial age. No one needs to know what a sea gull does or does not do. It's luxury knowledge. I've been offered a job at the Audubon Society for the rest of the summer. Let's get out of here and take it. I feel useless and sick at heart."

Luke got out of the car on the other side and walked down toward the water. The gulls were crying "Mew" and "Kleew" and "Hahahaha." Bright-footed sandpipers ran along the water's white edge, snatching pale crabs from the foam. The constant wind sang through the beach grass. He stood still and looked around.

Everything is the same, he thought. It shouldn't be. When someone dies there ought to be a big hole to show he's gone. Otherwise a person is like a candle burning. He vanishes, and there's nothing where he was.

His mother called and he struggled through the drifted sand to the gray lab. Mrs. Rivers was preparing coffee and toast, but Luke just wasn't interested. He went to his loft for his bathing trunks. He wanted to swim far out in the ocean and forget forever the sight of the falling jet. His father saw him and called, "Wait for me! I need a good hard swim, too."

He followed Luke down the sandspit, walking under a blanket. Luke was highly amused, but Dr. Rivers had learned how to fool the birds.

Luke dove headfirst into the other world beneath the surface of the sea. Flowerlike anemones opened and closed their tentacles, and bright-eyed fish tipped over to ogle him, then darted away. It occurred to Luke that life underwater was subject to its own grim laws—the big fish preyed on the little fish, and the little fish survived by flight. The seaweed rippled past his face, and a crab sallied out of it, flippers churning. Luke twisted and turned in the sea world until his lungs hurt, then surfaced with a blow.

"Nature's cruel," he said to his father, who swam with his nose just out of water. "I know all about the food chain and how the big fish eat the little fish who eat the littler fish. I know it's a fact, but I always feel sorry for the littlest fish." He laughed apologetically. "You'd think I wouldn't at my age."

Beyond his father's head Luke saw the ferryboat coming from Point Judith. Maybe this day would bring the letter from the National Science Foundation. It had been nine days since he had written. Luke quickly figured: three days to get there, three days to make a decision and five to process and check everything—three to get back—fourteen days. If it did not arrive today, he would not be disappointed. But he swam back to shore, dressed, and rode his bicycle to Old Harbor anyway.

There was no letter.

He started home, disappointed in spite of himself. As he passed the spring house tucked close behind Gregory's lobster shack, Luke felt Abnormality's absence. He was anxious to get away. Then he remembered Polly, Abnormality's pig.

The old spring house echoed emptily as Luke called "Sukie!" Abnor's life had been so simple there were no furnishings or clothes to dispose of. Polly was nowhere to be seen. The wind had taken possession of the house as if no one had ever lived there.

Luke's spirits dropped even lower, and he pushed his bike back to the road and slowly pedaled home. Then he remembered the island dump. He turned back, and steered down the bumpy dune road to what was surely the most interesting trash pile on the Atlantic coast—an acre of old washstands, Victorian dressers, walnut doors, and boat parts.

A huge gull was sitting authoritatively on an iron stove, but Polly was not in sight. Luke called "Sukie, sukie, sukie!" over and over again, but there was no answer. He couldn't waste any more time. His father wanted him to band young gulls during the afternoon, so he turned his bike homeward.

Out on the yellow beach he turned and called once more before riding away. There was a grunt. He called louder. The wind was in the right direction and evidently Polly had finally heard. She came huffing toward him over old boilers and stained-glass lampshades. When she reached him she squealed around him joyously, and Luke marveled that a beast that seemed as expressionless as a pig could have so much feeling.

"You'd better come home with me," he said to her. "I don't know what else to do with you." Polly squirmed and grunted in contentment as she followed him down the beach.

Luke stopped on the way to check the gullery. The

young were taking short flights down the dunes, while their parents called frantically from above their heads. The fledgling time of birds is a highly emotional time for parents.

A Navy jet ripped out of the sky. It frightened the pig and scattered the sea gulls. With a start, Luke looked frantically about for Spacecraft. This was just the chance he had been waiting for. His eyes fell on the bird hunched against the grasses at the bottom of the dune.

"Now I'm sure!" he said out loud. He noted down the time and the date, the movements, and the weather conditions. Grinning with success he jumped on his bike and pedaled down the beach. He could hardly wait to get to the lab.

"I think I know something!" he shouted as he burst through the door. "Spacecraft is afraid of jets. Maybe because I dropped him and hurt him the day he hatched. . . ." He jumped over the table and lifted out the file for "Spacecraft."

His father sat forward, raising his eyebrows at Luke's whirl of enthusiasm. "You may have something there," he said calmly. "Let's see." He took the notes. "Yes, yes, yes . . . hmm . . . there is one thing wrong. *You* are always there. It might be that he's afraid of you. And we don't have any controls. No notes when there aren't any jets flying over. Except one when there was thunder, but that's hardly a control, and it's only once. You may be right; but we can't prove it yet."

He looked up and said matter-of-factly, "Go back when there are no jets and take notes. Then take more notes when there are jets. I'll call the Naval airport and find out when the jets come over. You can be there every time. . . . Let's check it."

"Isn't this enough?" Luke said. His impatience was rising. He took the note cards and sifted through them. "Gee, I have seven, no, eight entries. I could write about it for the Wilson Bulletin with just this."

"No, not yet. You must be more thorough. You can't jump to conclusions."

Luke's impatience continued to rise. There seemed to be no end to research. Was some of it just research for the sake of going on? For never reaching conclusions?

"Nuts," he said. "I don't really want to find out." He clumped toward the kitchen for cookies and milk. An "oink, oink" at the door reminded him that he had a new responsibility.

"Hey, I found Polly and brought her home," he said.

His father came to the kitchen door. "What do we do with her?" he asked no one in particular. "I'm going to take that Audubon job soon and we'll be gone from here."

Luke looked curiously at his father. How could

he be so calm about putting behind him all the work on the gulls? He couldn't mean it. But his father's face was determined.

They stood in the kitchen door. Chinquapin walked in from the beach where she had been sunning and came over to join them. She gazed in amazement at Polly. His mother came down from the loft where she had been dusting and she, too, looked at the pig. "Well," she said, "I guess we have a pet." Luke could sense that they were each relieved as she patted the bristly head.

After dinner Dr. Rivers started packing his books. "Gee," Luke said, "are you really going to let five years' work go to waste?"

"It is not wasted," Dr. Rivers answered in flat tones. He set down an armload of books and spoke earnestly. "I've learned a great deal in these five years. For instance, by working with the gulls I have seen that the idea of nature as dog-eat-dog is all wrong. Nature is cooperative. It has to be, or there would be nothing left on earth but one super guzzling species. We are all alive on this earth because we have learned to live together, not because we have learned to fight. A few gulls spar, it's true, but for the sake of peace—not destruction. An occasional biff maintains order. We've been looking at nature wrong—seeing it from personal point of view. But look out there at the gulls and the terns and the crabs and fish living carefully with each other for the sake of living. To learn this has been worth five years." His voice had an air of finality, and he stood quietly at the window.

Luke stood beside his father and watched the gulls rise and fall as they settled down for the night. He was touched that his father had spoken to him in this manner, and he was sorry that the gull study was over. If only he could do something.

The next morning Luke was sent to the gullery to band as many juveniles as possible. It was hard, hot work. He had to catch the birds they had not banded as chicks, band them, weigh them, and measure their wings for growth records. Even though his father was packing to leave, he wanted the last odds and ends tied up.

Promptly at noon Luke came home and marked the band numbers on the map and the chart, bolted his lunch, and hurried to the wharf to meet the ferryboat. There was no letter.

He was desperate; there was so little time left. If only the scholarship would come, he could stop his father from giving up his work.

But by evening the cardboard heads were packed, and the tapping boxes were piled together. Luke's chest hurt to see what was happening.

"I wish we could wait a few more days . . . until
. . . well, maybe something will happen," he said.

"What could happen? Do you think my ship will
come in?" His father laughed. "No, I've made up my
mind. I've learned a lot on this study. And I've
published a few good articles on the work. It's time
to call a halt."

At noon the next day Luke stood on the wharf
awaiting the ferry. The sea was rough, and the boat
docked with bumps and knocks. The mail bag was
tossed into the postmaster's station wagon. Luke
biked behind the station wagon to the post office,
as he had every day for the past three days. This time
Mr. Sneider handed him the letter.

He tore it open and read only one sentence:

"We are sorry to inform you that your application
for a scholarship has been rejected. . . ."

That afternoon Chinquapin burst into the Sea
Bird Lab and breathlessly asked her father for ten
dollars at once. "The fishermen have taken up a
collection for Abnor," she said. "They're going to
hire a stonesmith to chip his name, his real name,
Andrew L. Comstock, on the big rock at the end of
the breakwater."

"That's nice," said Dr. Rivers calmly, and reached
for his wallet. Luke was surprised at the amount of
the bill he pressed into Chinquapin's hand. His

father must have been more deeply affected by Abnor's death than Luke had realized.

Mrs. Rivers said in a startled voice, "That's a lot, Frank. I think you should give in proportion to your income."

"Oh, let him give it if he wants to," quavered Chinquapin. "We'll all be gone tomorrow and we'll have lots of money again." Her voice was raising to a high pitch. "And it's all my fault, because I learned to swear at the docks." She covered her face and wept.

Mrs. Rivers put her arm around Chinquapin. "We're leaving because your father wants to—and for no other reason," she said soothingly. But the shoulders heaved and shook. Luke knew how Chinquapin felt. He, too, felt responsible for ending the study of the herring gulls at Block Island.

Early the next morning while they were at breakfast, there was a knock at the door. Luke's mother put down the frying pan and opened the creaking screen. The tall man who smiled down at her took off his cap and bowed slightly.

"I'm Fred Jarvis, from the Federal Aviation Agency. I'm looking for Dr. Frank Rivers."

"Dr. Rivers is here." She stepped back and let the big man enter.

He strode to Luke's father, and pumped his hand so hard Luke was embarrassed for them both.

"I understand you've been out here studying gulls for a number of years."

"Yes, I have."

"We need you—badly. Airways Flight 9 plunged into Boston Bay because sea gulls and starlings were sucked into her jets."

Dr. Rivers clutched the table. "Not sea gulls," he muttered. "That's too ironic."

"Well, starlings, too," Mr. Jarvis said. "And a black duck. All of them are guilty."

Luke rubbed his head. So the sea gulls killed him. The sea gulls, the beautiful white birds . . . Abnor had fed them . . . Mr. Jarvis had seated himself on one end of the slender bamboo chairs. Its legs were bowing under his weight. Luke stared at the chair and concentrated hard on whether or not it would break. After a few minutes he had pushed his thoughts of Abnor and the gulls to the back of his mind. He found himself listening with a new awareness.

Mr. Jarvis was addressing his father with great respect. "This isn't the first time gulls have been a nuisance. However, it's the first time there's been a fatal accident. It's unfortunate that it took this to show us that this is a problem that must be solved. Can you come with me to Logan Airport in Boston? Starlings chirp in the buildings, sea gulls loll on its runways, and there are some other little long-legged birds that run. . . . "

"Sandpipers. . . . " Dr. Rivers said.

"Yes, they run all over the airfield. Can you help us get rid of the birds? Will you come? The consultant fee is only fifty dollars a day, which isn't much when you're being pulled away from research . . . but . . . will you?"

"Yes, of course," Dr. Rivers said quickly. "I don't care about the money; I just want to help . . . I'll do it for nothing . . . after all . . . "

Luke sensed his mother's exasperation, and Luke was ready to shout at him. But Mr. Jarvis took over.

"I understand how you feel. But we'll have to pay you. You'll find it gives you authority to speak when you're connected with the United States government."

"I see. All right, when do you want me to begin?"

"Today. Now. Can you come to Boston with me this minute?"

Dr. Rivers smiled. "As a matter of fact," he said, "I'm all packed."

"Good." Mr. Jarvis grinned. "Let's go."

Dr. Rivers halted him. "One request," he said. "May I take my son Luke? There are some aspects of the behavior of the herring gull that he knows more about than I do."

"Very good," said Mr. Jarvis. "Glad to have him."

Luke could feel a glow rise from his toes and close over him. He turned abruptly and went up the ladder to his loft. As he stood before his orange-crate dresser planning what to take, shirts . . . pants . . . books . . . he tried to concentrate, but all he could think about was his father's remark. He said I knew a lot. He said I knew more about some things than he did!

He jerked a few clothes into a duffle bag, and closed the snap with confidence. With one hand he came down the ladder and stood tall beside his father. Out of the corner of his eye he noticed he only had two inches to grow to pass him. An affectionate warmth suffused him. "I'm ready, bird man," he said. "Let's go."

The Airport

A few Rebel gulls were circling the ferryboat when the men arrived at the dock. Larus shrieked out the warning, "Hahahaha," when he spotted Luke's father.

"Let's go inside," Dr. Rivers said, full of the memories of the last trip. Mr. Jarvis looked surprised, but he followed.

The gulls drifted beside the boat for several miles. They used the air currents around it to hold them aloft. Luke watched from the front of the ferry as the birds opened and closed their feathers like fingers against the wind.

The Airport

A mile out, the Block Island gulls turned back toward shore. For a few minutes there were no birds, and then the boat was met by an escort of gulls from the mainland.

At noon the Sea Bird Lab beach wagon drove into Logan Airport. The sky was full of gulls. They bent their pinions against the wind and soared and circled. As Luke stared at them he realized he was not looking at Larus and Spacecraft, individuals he knew, but a sky full of nature that had to be harnessed. Dams could be made to hold back floods, but what held back gulls? He bumped into his father, who had stopped short.

"Scuse me," Luke said and waited. An impressive-looking gray-haired man was on the steps to meet them. Luke wondered what there was about the man that made him look so important. Perhaps it was his stern nose and gray hair? Then Luke decided it was the way the man moved: he was sure of himself. He makes me feel like a rookie on the third team, Luke told himself.

Mr. Jarvis introduced them. "Mr. David," he began, "I want you to meet Dr. Rivers and his son, Luke." He turned to Dr. Rivers. "Mr. David is President of Airways." Airways owned the fateful Flight 9.

Mr. David wasted no time. "The company has a guest room here at the airport," he said. "It will be for your use while you're here." He smiled. "You can see the birds from all the windows first thing in the morning and last thing at night."

"Thank you," said Dr. Rivers and started for the steps. Luke was proud to see his father plunge forward with such determination. He wasn't going to waste words either.

Their room was enormous. It was hung with heavy curtains and carpeted with deep pile. The beds were high and beautiful. Luke had never seen such a room. He drifted past the men and stood in the middle. With some embarrassment he heard his father say, "This will make an adequate lab, but we'll need some big, long tables to work on."

But Mr. David did not seem to mind. "All right," he said, as if it were already accomplished, and added, "anything else?"

"I'd like to make a tour of the airport this afternoon. I'll need any maps you have of the area, and I suggest you hire about fifteen or twenty men to shoot off blank cartridges whenever the birds come in to roost. That will scare them off until we can solve the problem biologically."

"Fine, that will be done at once," Mr. David said, then added, "A car will be waiting for you downstairs when you're ready." They all shook hands and left.

Luke followed his father quietly to the jeep ordered by Mr. David. He started to say something funny to the driver about hunting dickey birds, but

131

he never said it. The driver was looking too respect-
ful. "Where first, sir?" he asked.

"The runways on the bay front."

For the next hour Luke watched his father take
notes. Buildings, grasses, rocks, and numbers of
people were noted. Slowly he realized that Block
Island and Logan Airport were different problems
that required different methods of study. His father
had known it all along.

When they got back to the airport office at five
o'clock, the maps were ready, as well as a dozen men
equipped with shotguns. Dr. Rivers made one more
request, for time schedules of all the flights that came
and left the airport. Mr. David flipped a button, and
his secretary brought in a sheaf of papers. Then
Luke's father took over. To the jeep driver he said,
"Put one man on each runway, beginning now until
dark." He passed a schedule to each of the men, and
said, When a flight is scheduled on your strip, blast
until all the birds are gone; and blast whenever they
come in to sit. We'll do this until we can get at something more basic."

When Luke and Dr. Rivers were back in their
luxurious room, Luke was impatient to discuss an
idea that had been nagging at the back of his mind
all afternoon. But before he could speak up, his
father was ordering him around, just as he had been
ordering men around at the airport office.

"Luke, I want you to get up at dawn with a clip

board full of these maps. Begin on strip seven and count the birds. I want the species, number, and the length of their stay on the strip. There will be more than gulls to recognize. Do you know your dowitcher and least tern?"

"I think so."

"I said, 'Do you?' "

"I will," Luke replied meekly. His mind went back to his Roger Tory Peterson. Why hadn't he packed it?

"Get the pattern of the movement of all the birds on this airport. You'll stick on this problem all day long and for the number of days it takes us to make some sense out of their habits. Remember, put down everything, relevant or irrelevant . . . the conclusions will take care of themselves.

"Tomorrow I'm going to fly over the entire Boston area in a helicopter. I want to see where all the birds are concentrated. I want to see the Lynn dump, the fishing piers, Marblehead, Cape Ann. I have to know why they fly from one place to another. Once I know why, it won't be so hard to break their routines."

Luke tried to grasp the enormous picture of birds from Maine to Connecticut. His father was not playing with dickey birds, but with movements of life as relentless as the rushing blaze of a forest fire.

He watched his father spreading maps on the table, and sat quietly, subdued by a whole new admiration for him.

The telephone rang.

"Lobster?" his father said into the 'phone. "Who's paying for it?"

Again Luke suffered embarrassment. There he goes, making another scene about money. But the agony died away as his father said firmly into the telephone, "No! I can't accept dinner from a chemical company. I know there's no obligation. I know I won't be influenced by a lobster dinner at the harbor. But if I happen to think chemicals will help solve this problem I don't want to be in the position of looking as if I were indebted to anyone. Thanks just the same."

Luke pulled his knees up and sat far back on the bed. The telephone rang again.

"The mayor of Boston? All right."

Luke unwrapped his legs and leaned forward.

"Yes. I have lots of suggestions. I'd also like to discuss the possibility of changing dumps and piers. If that fishing industry wasn't on the inner harbor, the gulls wouldn't sit on Logan airport and wait for the refuse. . . . When. . . . Tomorrow at nine. Fine." He hung up.

The telephone rang. It was the governor of the state.

"Of course you can help. We need a committee of the best men in the country; not only ornithologists but radar experts, chemists, physicists, and sociologists. Get Dr. James Reeves of Illinois; he's a

starling expert. We need him. The best man on shore
birds is Carl Sprinter in Washington. And get Frank
Allard at Northeast Harbor in Maine—he's the
authority on animal behavior. And it would be great
to have Jim Olsen from the University of Pennsyl-
vania here. He's the man who has been scaring starlings out of Philadelphia by taping their alarm
cries. . . . Yes, I'll be in your office at noon."

The world of birds was bringing the outside world
to Luke. He was astonished. "I didn't know you knew
so much about civilization," he said. "I thought you
only studied the tapping of gulls and little things
like that."

"Aha!" his father said. He raised his eyebrows.
"This is exactly what I've been trying to teach you.
Pure research gives you the background. If you begin
there—the rest is easy."

The telephone rang again.

"A dance in my honor?" Luke suppressed a snicker.
"No, I'm sorry," his father went on, "I don't think
I have time to sponsor a dance. But thank you very
much. And have a good time." He chuckled as he
hung up, and winked at Luke. "Maybe that's an
assignment for you."

"No sir." Luke was stern. "Not me."

Again the phone rang. "Yes, this is Dr. Rivers. The
Audubon Society? Oh, yes—the sea gull study."

Luke listened intently. Ha, they want him now.

Now they have money for him. He leaned forward.

"Yes, it certainly is ironic that yesterday's un-important study is today's crisis. Yes, thanks, I *can* use you. Have you a list of the loafing grounds of the herring gulls anywhere?" There was a pause while his father got a pencil. "Okay, go ahead. Rooftops near the fish piers . . . Atlantic Avenue, the Boston Basin, the Center excavation, Logan Airport, right! Splendid! I'll fly over these areas tomorrow and see if they can be made even more attractive to the gulls. If we could lessen the attractiveness of the airport and make these other places the most desirable loafing grounds in the gull world, we'd be on our way." He laughed. "And Larry, where are the gulleries—the nesting sites, in the area?" He spoke the names aloud as he wrote. "The islands in the outer harbor. Green, Little Calf, the Brewsters, and Lovell. Splendid. Thanks." He hung up. "Luke, let's eat and go to bed," he said. "You must be up at four."

They went to the airport snack bar for hamburgers and then back to their room.

"You know, it's funny," Luke said as they were undressing, "last week I resented it when you told me what to do. You made me feel like a little toddler. Now, I don't mind it. At last I know why."

"Why?" Dr. Rivers asked from the smooth percale sheets.

"Because you're yelling at me as if I were another

one of the men on the job. I don't feel like your son—and I like it."

"Well, on this job you're not my son. No special favors, no ignoring poorly done work. Now get some sleep."

"Okay." Luke put his head down. The events of the day whirled through his mind. Conversations with mayors and governors . . . a far cry from life with the gulls on Block Island.

Spacecraft

Two mornings later a sharp knock on the door cata-
pulted Luke from his bed before his 4:30 alarm went
off. The July sun was still below the horizon. He
swung open the oak door to greet a tall, lean man,
with a shock of white hair, sharp blue eyes, and a
grinning, ruddy face.

"Hi-yah!" the man shouted and shook Luke's
hand. "You're Luke, aren't you? I'm Jim Olsen, a
fellow ornithologist. Where's your father?"

Luke pointed to the mound in the other green bed.

"Frank Rivers!" Long legs carried the skyscraper-
like figure across the room.

Luke's father blundered out of bed and stumbled forward. "Jim Olsen!" he said delightedly. "I've wanted to meet you for years. I've read all your findings in the Auk Magazine. Now that you're here the problem is well in hand."

While Dr. Rivers was in the dressing room, Dr. Olsen seated himself firmly at the table and studied the maps of the airport. Luke watched him open an attaché bag decisively and take out a small tape-recording machine.

"Hahahaha-hahaha," rang out as he started the tape moving. Luke grinned. He understood immediately what Dr. Olsen was up to. By playing tapes of the alarm cry of the gulls he would scare them off the airstrips.

"That's great," his father said as he came into the room tying his tie. "Will a loud-speaker broadcast this?"

"No. I'm going to put a small speaker on each runway. Up in the tower, the departure engineer checks the time, flicks on the tape—away go the birds—off go the jets."

Luke liked Dr. Olsen's energy, his expressive hands, his deep voice. He liked the idea of the tapes and said so. His father was more cautious. He listened to the tape three or four times.

"When did you record the 'hahaha's,' " he asked.

"Just last week," Dr. Olsen replied.

"I thought so. The nesting season is well along. The tape doesn't sound as frantic as it could."

"Don't you think it will work?"

"For a few days at the most, maybe. Then I think the Boston gulls will catch on."

There it was again—Luke wondered why his father always had to be so critical. Dr. Olsen was an important man, and Luke thought his father was presuming too much. Luke snatched his clip board, twisted his binoculars over his head, and went out the door. As he left he heard Dr. Olsen booming into the telephone to the ground engineers, "Get ready for a new kind of show!"

His irritation at his father simmered down as he ate his breakfast. Perhaps criticism was part of a scientist's world. It had not seemed to bother Dr. Olsen one way or another. Luke sighed. It would be wonderful to be old enough to give and take.

Stuffed with waffles and ham, Luke started work just at sun-up. At noon he went to the conning tower to report. He was discouraged. The birds he had been told to watch were gone.

He entered the tower cautiously. Four men sat around the core of windows watching radar screens, listening to radios, and keeping an eye on the airport below.

Luke could see all the runways, the bay, the birds,

and the horizon of buildings that was Boston. The "beeps" and the staccato radio voices filled the room with confusing noises. Everyone seemed to be able to concentrate, but Luke couldn't imagine how. He spoke to the nearest man.

"Hello, I'm Luke Rivers. I'm with the bird study."

"Hi! Carl Moody is the name. We know all about you fellows. We'll be glad to give you any help we can." He smiled. "I'm arrivals controlman. Hold on a minute—a jet's coming in from Washington—I'll be right with you." He turned to the control panel and bantered with the pilot as together they brought the big ship down on Runway 7.

"Number 7 is the gull's loafing strip," Luke said. "They're supposed to be there now, but I can't find them—two thousand of them."

"I guess the gunmen cleared them off. They seem to be pretty effective so far."

Luke peered out of the glass windows with his binoculars. Slowly he made a complete circle. Then he said, "Mind if I try to find my birds on that radar screen? A flock of five hundred came in from the piggeries. For the last two days they've been sitting on Runway 7 at noon. Then they go northeast toward Chelsea, but today I've lost them."

"Let's try," Carl said. As they sat before a vast panel of lights and dials, he pushed the buttons that regulated the radar. Slowly the screen filled with lights. Carl studied them. None of the flashes said "birds" to the expert.

Once more Luke scanned the airport with his binoculars. "There they are!" he shouted. "On 12!" He had spotted the two thousand missing gulls loafing on Runway 12.

"No!" gasped the departures controlman. "And Flight 405 is coming down to that strip right now."

Luke felt panic rising in him. What could be done? Then suddenly, as if on signal, the sea gulls flapped their wings and left; the airstrip was clean. They banked in the sun away from the oncoming jet and winged south like a silver army.

"Can't figure that out," Carl said on a sigh of relief.

Luke peered through his binoculars and watched them trail off into the bay. Far out over the misty water they folded their wings and came down.

"Saved by the garbage of Boston," he laughed. "They knew it was scow time and met the boat."

Carl stood up and took Luke's glasses. "Sure enough, they aren't so dumb," he marveled.

Luke sat down and wrote. Then he studied his notes. The notes didn't make sense. He knew where all the terns and ducks and gulls were. He knew when and where they flew. But just when he thought he had something for his father, just when he could see a pattern, two thousand of them got up and did something else.

"You know, Carl," he said, "I don't think we're getting anywhere."

"You people from all those universities sure know a lot about birds."

"But it's not helping anybody." Luke looked again at his notes. "You know," he said in a rush of confidence, "if what my father says is right, then I should go back to Block Island to work on this problem. I know a bird out there named Spacecraft. He's scared of jets. In fact, he sits and hides when he hears one. He's the fellow who could solve this whole problem. All we need is two thousand gulls who are scared of jets."

"He sounds great," Carl said. He winked. "Can he teach?"

"That's not as funny as you think," Luke said. "Birds teach their young."

For an hour he sat quietly in the tower counting and noting the birds that came by. He drew them on maps, marked where they went, and what they were doing.

"It's great up here," he said to the controlman between planes. "This beats hiking around looking for birds. Whoops, there goes a crowd of starlings off to the south." He stood up. "Where'd they go?"

Carl turned on the radar, dialed in on the flock and calculated where they had disappeared. "The marshes to the south of here," he declared.

Luke noted the place on his pocket map. "I may become the first birdman to gather data by radar."

Carl laughed. "And I may be the first engineer to be an assistant nature man."

They followed the movements of a flock of sea gulls from the bay. "You read the screen, I'll map them," Luke said.

"Wait'll I tell the Society of Engineers about this!" Carl said as he turned to the radar.

Luke glanced up from his maps and looked out the window to see his father and Dr. Olsen with a crew of men in an open jeep moving slowly down a runway. They were going to test the alarm cries of the gulls.

It would have been fun to join them, but he had been assigned to a job. He lifted his binoculars and studied the flying sandpipers. It's just like life on Block Island, he thought. Gather the data, write down the facts. Do it again and do it again. But things are different here, he mused, the facts are useful.

Luke came to dinner a few minutes late. The airlines had reserved a small table for the scientists, but within a few days, a large one had been set aside because their numbers had swelled from two to seven.

As Luke stood beside his father's chair, he smiled into two new faces.

His father performed introductions. "This is my son, Luke—Dr. Murra, a sociologist who has come to see whether fishing villages and piggeries can be moved—and Dr. Allard." He turned to Luke. "You've read Dr. Allard's papers."

"Yes," Luke breathed in admiration. He shook hands, then sank stiffly into a chair beside his father, conscious of the long-nosed, gentle-looking man on the other side of him.

Dr. Olsen bellowed out across the table, "Good evening, Luke! Did you get the birds to bed?"

"Yes, sir," Luke replied. "How are the tapes?"

"Oh, we're still setting up the speakers."

The waiter arrived, orders were placed, and the conversation nestled down to low murmurs between pairs of men. Luke wanted desperately to speak to Dr. Allard, but he did not know what to say to so famous a man. Finally, he took a deep breath and blurted out, "Dr. Allard, do you think birds could be frightened so badly when they hatched that they would stay away from airports all their life?"

Dr. Allard turned to Luke with a direct, kindly gaze. "Fear certainly affects their behavior. What do you have in mind?"

Luke felt his knees shaking. He did not know whether he could go on in the presence of such greatness. But Dr. Allard's eyes were warm upon him and he took courage.

"One day last spring, I helped a chick from an egg —gull number 737. When a jet screamed overhead I dropped the chick—and hurt him. All my notes after that date show that he goes into a trance and hides when a jet goes overhead."

"Fascinating!" Dr. Allard said. "Do you have many such notes?"

"Eight or nine."

"That's enough to make a good paper. Very interesting—you ought to write it up."

Luke's food was brought to the table but he could scarcely eat it. He kept his eyes on Dr. Allard's balding head and long New England nose, and described his adventures with Spacecraft.

"Interesting, very interesting," Dr. Allard mumbled as he listened. "You ought to drop other chicks, perhaps out here at the airport when jets take off— see if this can be repeated. I can see possibilities in frightening whole populations to avoid certain sounds. In fact," he said suddenly, "I think you should go on with this research."

Luke felt as though he were smiling from his insides out. He knew now what it meant to be inspired.

At the end of the meal he caught his father at the door. "Dad," he said, "I want to go back to Block

Island and study Spacecraft. Dr. Allard thinks maybe we can frighten chicks the way I frightened Spacecraft. Maybe we could condition them all to stay away from airports." His excitement was mounting.

Then it happened.

His father was in a hurry; the experiments with the tapes were immediate. His father's hand came up and patted him on the head. Luke was reduced to a little boy. He froze and pulled away. "Run along now, Lukie, and get some sleep," his father said. "We need more maps of the bird highways and byways."

And Dr. Rivers followed the other men through the big doors into the night.

Luke went back to the table. "Lukie! Lukie!" He pinched his nose between his eyes to stop the pain of the insult. He pulled the chair out roughly and sat down on it hard, thrusting his head into his fists. His anger was almost overwhelming. Why had everything been so nice the other day? Why had his father treated him as a man then? Was it because he had kept his neck in, like the little herring gulls and was doing what his father wanted? I just wanted to talk straight to him, he thought, and what does he do? Humiliate me. "Lukie!"

The waitress started to clear off the table. "Are you through, sir?" she asked.

Luke glanced up quickly, savoring the "sir." "Yes, thanks," he said firmly. He left the dining room with a sense of relief and melting anger, and looked at the airstrips lit with beams of light. His day tomorrow would start at 4:30. He *did* need his sleep.

During the next few days he counted and mapped and worked from dawn to dusk. But he often wondered where he was and what he was doing. He was sure that Spacecraft was the answer to the problem of how to get birds off airports. And the more he thought about Spacecraft, the more he felt he should go back to Block Island and find him. But his father would not let him go.

Day after day he marked down flights and habits. Dr. Allard was studying the gulleries to see if they could be sprayed in the nesting season with a chemical that would kill the embryos. Dr. Murra, the sociologist, was working with him, for the people of Boston were becoming a major factor in the problem. They were now taking the birds' side; they did not want their gulls killed, in or out of eggs. And Luke continued to count and map.

Nine days of work passed by. It was almost the middle of July. The gunmen were doing an excellent job of keeping the runways clear of birds until the scientists could complete their research. Everyone was working steadily and hard. Finally, the survey began to bear fruit.

Dr. Murra leaned on the dining table at noon on

the ninth day and said to Luke's father, "I've done all I can do. My work's done. I've surveyed the possibility of changing certain industries, but without success. And today I tried to get the mayor to move the fishermen out of the Inner Bay as you suggested."

"What'd he say?" asked Dr. Rivers.

"He hit the ceiling. Said it was a marginal industry and would collapse if moved. He also added, 'and I wouldn't get re-elected.'"

Dr. Rivers shook his head. "So the birds have got us into politics!"

"I never thought we might affect an election," roared Dr. Olsen. "We certainly are naive."

Dr. Murra went on. "The same is true of the dumps and the piggeries. It would cost too many votes to move them. Pity."

"And what about spraying the roosts of the starlings and gulls?" asked Dr. Rivers.

"The bird lovers would put such pressures on all the civic organizations that you'd never get any more funds."

Luke watched his father's face.

"Well," said Dr. Rivers thoughtfully, "we'll have to change the environment, then. Why don't we cover up the beaches with something that looks like a forest and cut the grass at Logan Airport?"

"That's your area," said Dr. Murra, "but the people can't be changed."

Luke listened hard. The problem was presenting a complexity he'd never dreamed of. He turned to Dr. Allard. "I guess Spacecraft and his fear of jets is the best idea after all," he said.

Dr. Allard put his rough hand over Luke's. "It may take years, but the possibility should be studied," he said. "I mean it."

The next morning, after a week of installation and pretesting, the first gull calls were to be tested. Luke and Dr. Rivers were up early. Several scientists from Washington and three presidents of airlines would be present to see if the device was going to work. His father had said Luke might join the group and he felt a sneaking pride that he was to be the youngest witness to this important experiment.

Luke dressed quickly, and his father took so long getting ready that Luke decided to go to the dining room and start breakfast. He ordered a big glass of orange juice and was adding bacon, eggs, and waffles to the list when Dr. Allard entered the empty room. Luke's heart beat fast. He did so admire the kindly scientist.

"Good morning, Luke," Dr. Allard called to him.

Luke stood up, knocking his silverware to the floor as he jerked his hand forward in greeting.

"Are you ready for the big test?" Dr. Allard inquired.

"Of course," Luke said. "It's exciting."

Dr. Allard ordered a breakfast almost as big as

Luke's, then stretched back in his chair. "Do you think it'll work?" he asked Luke seriously.

"Not for long," Luke answered. He felt very sure of himself.

"Why not?"

"Dad thinks the calls are too weak. Dr. Olsen had to make tapes late in the nesting season, when the gulls are less wary. The tapes will scare them off for a few days, but then I'll bet a dollar these smart old Boston gulls will catch on and come right back to loaf on the airstrips."

"You know a lot for a young man," Dr. Allard said.

"I learned it by osmosis," Luke chuckled. "I've worked with my Dad so long that I know a good full-blown alarm cry when I hear one. As a matter of fact, my Dad can get a more violent cry in any season than the cry on these tapes. All he has to do is walk out the lab door, and the 'hahas' are fierce. Sometimes I think they can be heard in England."

"Why is that?" Dr. Allard asked curiously.

"Well, it's a family joke that Dad is the most hated man on Block Island. He has more enemies than anyone we know—all gulls. He has invaded their nesting sites so much that they regard him as their chief enemy. Those tapes should have been made with Dad on the Block Island gullery, head bare, coat off."

"Hmmmmm," said Dr. Allard. "Have you spoken to Dr. Olsen about this?"

"No, I never thought of it 'til just now."

"I'm sure that's just what should be done. If this tape fails, I'll recommend your idea." Dr. Allard looked thoughtful, then he said, "By the way, Luke, write down your experiment with Spacecraft. I'm on the college committee for the National Science Foundation. Some of my colleagues ought to see what you're doing on Block Island. Write down your premise—to see if birds can be conditioned to react to sounds by frightening them early in life—then tell how you would go about developing this. Send it to me."

"Thank you, sir. I would like to do that." Luke bit his lower lip to keep it from trembling with excitement.

While they were eating, the sky had lightened. In the faint light of dawn, seven men and a boy climbed to the conning tower high above Logan Airport. They checked their watches, lifted their binoculars, and waited. At 4:45 A.M. Airways Flight 11 was to take off for Washington, D.C.

The jet was loaded and standing by at 4:40. It was ready to taxi down gull-filled Runway 7. Luke saw through his binoculars that all his white and gray friends, almost eight hundred of them, were just awakening on the airstrip. Some preened, others began to gossip in soft "mew" voices.

"Flight 11 to tower," the jet captain said over the

radio. "We're ready to take off. Let the birdies sing."

"Tower to Flight 11. Okay. I'm starting the tape. Give it two minutes to run and two minutes more. Then start. I'll keep you informed."

Engineer Carl Moody flicked the switch on the tape recorder at his left. The gull alarm cry could not be heard in the tower; the scientists could only see what was happening. They all lifted their binoculars and stared at the small speakers on the runway.

Around the boxes birds looked to the right and left. They got on their wings. More got up. Then more and more until in three minutes the whole flock was flying out over the bay.

"They're leaving," the departure controlman said to the pilot of Flight 11. "They're leaving! Hold your engines until the air is clear."

"Are they really flying away?" the pilot burst back with a laugh.

"Can't you see them go?" the tower replied.

"They're too low. Yes! Now I can see them against the waters of the bay. I'll be durned."

"Okay, go!" shouted the radio man. The jet screamed forward and sped down Runway 7.

"Beautiful day!" the pilot cried. "And not a bird in the sky!"

The jet sprang off the ground, and then, gaining speed, shot swiftly up above Boston Bay.

"Bravo!" the men in the conning tower shouted.

Spacecraft

But when the shouts had died down and the laughter abated, above the buzz of radios and the tick of clocks Dr. Olsen's voice boomed out, "I'll save my shouts for a month from today. These Boston birds are no dunces!"

The Fledgling

Luke tosssed his shirt into the fancy green laundry basket that stood in the bathroom. "Dad," he said, "I sure wish you'd let me go home and study Spacecraft. I could watch him for the rest of the summer and get quantitative data. Maybe next year we could raise a whole mess of Spacecrafts."

His father's voice was raspish. "How often must I tell you! The idea is much too impractical. One bird doesn't prove anything. And I need you here. What we're doing here is far more important."

"But I'm not doing any good here. Please, let me go back."

"No. And that's final. I need you. Let me be the judge of whether or not you're doing any good here."

"But what about me? I'm sure I'm right. Even Dr. Allard thinks I might have something."

"Luke, you're young." Luke tensed as his father crossed the floor and stood in front of him. "You don't know enough zoology, or heredity, much less chemistry and psychology, to judge your idea. Science is not a fly-by-night affair . . . it is a long struggle to learn and interpret. I say no. I want you to promise me you'll drop this."

Luke closed his eyes. His fingers closed so tightly that his nails dug his palms. "I will *not* promise." He stood still to face the consequences of what he'd said.

His father stopped buttoning his shirt. "Luke," he said firmly. "You promise me!"

"You mean promise not to go back to Block Island?"

"That is correct. I want the study of the bird population here completed. You will finish that?"

"I don't think I will," Luke said quietly. "I don't think it's worth a tinker's dam." His knees shook slightly at his boldness.

His father's face flushed an angry red. "Luke," he said in a controlled, furious voice, "I choose to ignore the fact that you have spoken to me in this manner. The matter is closed. You will do as you are told. I do not want to hear one more word on this subject."

With that he turned and left the room, closing the door firmly behind him.

All morning Luke wandered the airport, counting the birds and marking them down on his maps. He was too unhappy to do a good job. After three hours he sat down to think things over.

I guess Dad's right, I don't know enough and I'm better off here, he said to himself. He waited to see if being a good, obedient son would make him feel better. It didn't.

Late in the afternoon he climbed to the conning tower to track a flock of sandpipers he had lost.

"How's the tape working?" he asked Carl Moody.

"Haven't you heard?" he said.

"No, I've been chasing sandpipers and ducks. What's happened?"

"The gulls all walk over to the speaker box and stand around. They listen in fascination to the gull in the box. They love him!"

"No! no! Aren't they afraid any more?"

"Not in the least."

Luke turned and jumped down the steps. He had to find his father and Dr. Olsen. They were out on Airstrip 4 trying to get a new "hahahaha" tape. He ran all the way, following the beach that flanked the airstrips.

A club of gulls was sitting along the beach. A few

were stretching their necks to see who was boss. Some were sleepily contemplating their feet. As he approached Airstrip 3, a warning yell behind him announced that a jet was about to take off. Luke ran into the weeds and lay down. He hated to be so close to the awful noise, but better on the ground than standing.

As he lay curled on his side, he could see three gunmen who had been posted along the bay stand up and shoot off blank cartridges. They were back to the old method of scaring gulls. The guns boomed, the birds flew away, and the jet ripped forward.

Just as it was getting off the ground Luke sat up straight. A gull had run into the grasses to hide.

Once the jet was aloft, Luke ran swiftly to the bird. It was hiding . . . from the noise, Luke hoped. He lunged for it. The bird took off. Flat on his chest Luke watched it fly away. It was missing a third left primary feather, and a second right tail feather.

"I'll get you," he shouted. "No matter what Dad says, I want you!"

At dinner that night he told Dr. Allard about the gull that hid from the noise. Dr. Allard's blue eyes widened. "Can you catch him?" he asked.

"Sure, if I had time . . . Dad and I often trap them in nets to band them."

"Any identifying marks so you'd know it again?"

"Yes, it was with B gull club, and it was missing a

left primary feather, and a right tail feather. There can't be many with that combination."

"Good, good, that's good," Dr. Allard said. "If you don't mind, I'd like to help you net it. I spent all of today going over different compositions to be used on the runways. Chemists are trying to find an airstrip covering that will hurt the birds' feet. Nothing promising yet . . . and I'm tired of being inside."

Luke could hardly believe his good fortune. He cleared his throat. "That would be fine, sir."

"Good," said Dr. Allard. "I'll meet you tomorrow at three. We'll try to get that gull." He paused, then added with a twinkle, "Let's hope it's a female. If so, we'd really be in luck. Maybe it could be a mate for Spacecraft. If so, we'll find out if parents can teach fear."

Luke was so excited he didn't trust his voice to speak. He just nodded.

"By the way," Dr. Allard said suddenly, "I hope it's a juvenile."

"It is—why?"

"Adults mate for life and it's pretty hard to breed them in captivity if you break up a mated pair."

"And Spacecraft's a juvenile too," Luke affirmed.

At nine o'clock that night Luke was still excited. He went over the maps and counts of the day, but found it was hard to concentrate.

"You've made several mistakes in adding," his father said, and changed the totals.

The next afternoon Luke and Dr. Allard walked out to Airstrip 5, where B club of gulls was loafing. They hid in the grass with a net on a long pole and watched the jets take off. No bird ran into the grass, and they saw no bird missing number three left primary and number two right tail feather. Luke went back to counting birds. Dr. Allard returned to the office to examine new materials for runways.

The next day Luke's father flew to Philadelphia with Dr. Olsen to bring back some better recordings of gulls. As he departed, three ornithologists from the south arrived at Logan to band gulls. They were going to find out whether it was just a local gull group which sat on the airports or gulls from Cape Cod and Boston and the islands. They went to work quietly and swiftly. The information was needed right away.

Luke continued to count and map. But he could not stop thinking about Spacecraft and the strange gull he had seen hide in the grass.

Late that afternoon he decided to see what the banding party was doing. He found them along the bay. They had large snap nets set on the loafing grounds. When the birds came in to sit, a man hidden behind a rock jerked a cord which carried the net overhead and down upon the gulls. Luke sat down to watch.

The sun was hot. The three men had just trapped about seventy-five flopping birds in one of their nets. They were banding the birds as fast as they could. One by one they took the birds from the tangle of threads, put bands on their legs, and set them free. Luke saw they were fairly skillful, but they didn't know how to keep from being bitten. They tried to hold the beaks closed with their hands. He was about to go over and tell them to put rubber bands on the beaks when one man suddenly spun and dove. He had almost lost a bird. It fluttered in his hand, one wing flapping hard on the air. The second primary was missing; Luke jumped to his feet and tore across the runway.

"Mister! Mister!" he called. "Don't let that bird go! Please hold him!"

His heart was thumping—and not just from running.

"May I see that bird please? I must have it!"

"Do you have a collector's license?" demanded the man.

"My father does. I'm Luke Rivers. My father is working on this problem, too."

"What's he want this bird for?"

Luke took a deep breath to keep from speaking too agitatedly. "Dr. Allard wants it," he said. "That

very bird. He wants to study its behavior. Can I take
it to him?"

"How do you know he wants this particular bird?"

"Let me see its tail."

The ornithologist spread the feathers.

"Yes! That bird!" Luke's hands involuntarily went
around the big fat bird and held it tightly.

"This bird," the ornithologist said firmly, "is my
responsibility. It's a migrating bird and the rules are
strict. I can't give it to unauthorized personnel." He
shook Luke's hands away, and turned to throw the
bird onto the air.

Luke was beside himself with frustration. Too
young, too unknowledgeable to be trusted! But of
course the man was right. He had captured the bird
and according to his permit he could use it only for
scientific study. He did not know Luke at all.

In desperation, he said, "If you don't believe me,
will you hold the bird until I get Dr. Allard? You
won't be sorry."

The ornithologist halted his movement and looked
at Luke speculatively. "All right," he said. "Go get
him. I'll wait."

The ornithologist tucked the bird tightly under
his arm. At that the bird swung its strong neck
around and bit him. "Ouch!" he cried. "I can't hold
it. The durn thing bites." He turned again to re-
lease the bird.

"Wait!" Luke said. He reached in his pocket,

fumbling through the papers and buttons until he found a rubber band. He slipped it over the gull's beak. "We always wrap handkerchiefs around the wings and bodies of the birds we want to hold," Luke said. "Then they can't flap and break their feathers." He began to tie the wings down with his own handkerchief. His hands were gentle. The ornithologist held the bird until it was secure.

"You know what you're doing," he said. "Take the bird to Dr. Allard."

"Thanks." Luke grinned and tucked the big sea gull under his arm. "I appreciate it. And when you see Dr. Allard tonight, I'm sure he'll thank you too."

His sense of triumph speeded him back to the terminal building. The gull eyed him with anger.

"I think he's a girl, I think he's a girl," Luke was mumbling happily. "The eyes are low, and the face is soft and feminine looking. Oh, I hope he's a girl."

He hurried to his room and put the gull in the closet. It would not be frightened in the dark. Then he telephoned several offices to locate Dr. Allard. He was in the conning tower.

"Oh, hi, Luke," he said kindly when Luke finally got hold of him.

"I've got the bird that hid when the jets flew over!" Luke shouted into the telephone. "I think it's a girl. I think I can maybe breed her and get jet-scared gulls!"

Luke's heart sank at the long silence at the other

end. Finally Dr. Allard spoke. "Luke," he said, "can you catch Spacecraft?"

"Catch Spacecraft! Sure."

"Do you have your notes on him?"

"Not here."

"Well, I think you should get them. Write all this down immediately and give it to me. And I think you should catch Spacecraft at once."

"Except Dad won't let me. He'll get mad at me."

Dr. Allard chuckled. "And are you afraid of wrath?"

Luke was still awake when his father returned from Philadelphia in the morning. He greeted Luke with a tired smile. "It looks as if we may have to go to Holland. The Dutch use tape recordings successfully. We may have to study them. Ours are so bad."

Luke hardly heard what his father was saying. He was concentrating too hard on his own words.

"Dad . . . ."

His father's voice was irritated. "What?" he snapped.

"I . . . how was your trip?" Luke had to change the subject. He could feel the perspiration stand out on his face. Maybe it would be easier just to slip out and leave a note. Then he wouldn't have to face his father's anger.

The idea made Luke feel better. He crawled back

into bed. His father was still answering his question about the trip, but Luke did not hear.

Suddenly his father, seated on the edge of his bed untying his shoes, looked like a large man—much larger than Luke had thought.

"Maybe I could take you to Holland if I go," his father said as he bent his knee and heaved off a shoe. "You could record the data for me and help keep notes."

"When will you go?" Luke asked stiffly.

"In a few days."

Luke gathered his courage, rolled over on his pillow, and with his back to his father said, too loudly, "I can't go."

There was a long pause. Then crisply and with authority, his father said, "Why not?"

Luke turned slowly around. "I'm going to Block Island tomorrow and catch Spacecraft. I'm going to study that bird!"

"Don't be ridiculous, Luke," his father said. Luke could tell that his father did not believe he would do such a thing.

"I'm leaving tomorrow," Luke repeated.

"No, you're not. You're here on a job. Now stop bothering me with all this nonsense and get on with the work . . . good night."

And Dr. Rivers climbed into bed with the air of a man who had won.

But before his father could put out the light Luke got out of bed and walked over to him. "We'd better talk, Dad. Because I'm going to do this. I am. I have to."

His father sat up and looked wearily at Luke. "Look, Luke," he said, "even if you do have a good idea it would take years to get anywhere with it."

"Well, you worked for years, for heaven's sake!" Luke said.

"I know, but . . . that's different. You're still young."

"So much the better. I've got to start some day. It might as well be now."

"Luke, I'm tired. I'll argue this in the morning." Suddenly he straightened up. "What's that noise?"

"A gull. It's in a box in the closet. It's fed, it's bound, and it's comfortable."

"What's it doing there?" His voice rose in annoyance.

"This bird hides in the grass when jets go over," Luke answered quietly.

Dr. Rivers set his jaw. "Luke, this is final. If you go against my will you won't be paid the money you've earned on this study. It comes to quite a bit. I'm sorry, but if you leave you will not have earned it."

His father turned out the lights, rolled over, and

went to sleep. But there was no sleep for Luke. Should he defy his father and follow his great awakening interest, or be sensible and stay? The thoughts in his head went around and around. After all, my father is a great man. I can learn much from him. I already have. He's a good and wonderful man. I should do what he wants.

At three o'clock Luke stuffed both fists into his pillow. But he makes me so mad.

The stars were sinking low when Luke wiped the sweat from his forehead and relaxed. He had decided to stay. His father would like that. He would be pleased. Luke wanted to please his father. He could feel his father's arm on his shoulder. He could see the pride in his father's face, when Luke said, "I'll stay and help." He could see his classmates and teachers smiling because Luke had obeyed his father.

He smiled at his own nobleness as he put his head down for what he hoped was sleep. But his eyes still would not close. A feeling more powerful than "being good" was taking hold of him. It forced him to lift his head and stare through the dimly lit night at his father. It made him see that his father was not as large in stature as he had seemed a few hours ago. It made him see that his father was not perfect; in fact, it seemed to him that his father was quite a self-centered and blind man.

The new thought hurt. He must not feel that way. After all, Dr. Rivers was his father. He must be loyal to him.

But he does get all wrapped up in his work to the exclusion of everyone else, Luke said to himself.

A searchlight on the field below illuminated his father's face for a moment. He's not as handsome as I used to think, either. Can't see why everyone says, "Your good-looking father. . . ." Heck, his nose is really much too crooked to look right, and his cheeks sag.

When the sun finally arose, Luke put on his good suit and packed. His father awakened at the sound of the alarm and sleepily stumbled to the dressing room.

When he came out, Luke was waiting for him, suitcase in one hand, big sea gull tucked under the other arm.

"Where are you going?" his father asked.

"I told you. Back to Block Island."

His father bent his shoulders back and roared. The laughter rolled out of him. "All right, now, put the bird down," his father said. "You've proved your point. Let's get on with the work."

Luke walked slowly toward the door. He felt quite calm, ready for the final clash with his father. Dr. Rivers turned and picked up some papers. Luke reached the door. He went through it, stepped out into the corridor, and walked to the top of the steps.

Then he ran. He ran as fast as he could down the stairs, across the terminal floor, and out the door to the bus.

In town, he walked to the railroad station. Passers-by laughed at the boy with the gull under his arm. Luke tried not to notice them. He had just stepped out of his father's image of him . . . a nice little boy . . . and he was finding the new suit of manhood a loose garb to wear.

The Jet Birds

As he walked down the long, lonely beach to the Sea Bird Lab Luke was delighted that the sky was clear. He heard the sea singing softly at his feet. Over the black lighthouse floated the beautiful sea gulls of Block Island.

He rounded the lab and stopped to look at Yank Hill. The wind was blowing, duning the sand and bending the grasses. The bird under his arm crooked its neck and listened to the voices of the gullery.

The front door flew open and Chinquapin rushed out. "Luke! When did you get back?"

He dropped his bag and hugged her self-consciously with his free arm. "Just this minute," he said, and smiled at her. He felt tall and relaxed in the warm sun of Block Island. "I'm going to run an experiment of my own."

"Oh, how wonderful." Her feet were planted firmly apart, like a child's. Luke heard no tease in her voice, just acceptance. "Who's the bird?" she asked.

"Oh, she's part of the experiment." Luke answered. "I think I'll call her Jetser. Want to help?"

"Sure—if I can."

"We've got to catch Spacecraft," he said and squinted into the sunny dune.

"I saw him yesterday at Old Harbor. He can fly like a bird!"

"What time was it?"

"About noon, I guess. We were shopping."

"We'll go over at noon tomorrow. Did you see his bands?"

"Yes, and I saw Larus, too. Luke, I think he's getting ready to migrate."

"No, not yet." He could hear the authority in his own voice. He picked up his suitcase and the bird and went into the lab. Chinquapin followed. "Where's Mother?" Luke asked.

"She went out to gather blackberries. We've made lots of jam while you all were gone." She struck an

171

impish pose. "You all won't let us do men's work, we'll do women's work. It was fun." She showed him the jars, then said, "I'll go get her." She ran out the door calling.

Luke went to work. He had gathered enough two-by-fours to make a walk-in cage when his mother came home.

He was glad to see her. Only then did he realize how much he had missed her.

"Lukie, dear," she said. "I'm so glad you're home. I want to hear all about your father . . . He writes so little. But before you relax, there's some chores to do. The stove needs cleaning and the screen door is jammed. Will you do them first, please?"

"I'll fix them later. I've gotta finish this first. Jetser needs a home."

"But Luke. I've waited for days for these things to be done. Now please come."

Luke walked to his mother and took her small shoulders in both hands. "I *will* do these things for you, but not now. This comes first."

"Oh, you men are all alike," she said sharply. "I'll do it myself."

Luke grinned. His mother had always been able to call him from baseball, study—anything, by saying with great offense, "I'll do it myself." "You sit right there while I finish my work," he said now. "Then

I'll help you." He was surprised at his own firmness. He turned away and picked up his hammer.

His mother chuckled, "Guess my tricks won't work anymore. You're getting insight, Luke."

He glanced at her quickly. A fellow's parents, he thought, have many different faces as he grows up. There sits my mother, once the center of the universe, the most wonderful and most beautiful person in the world. All of a sudden she's just another person struggling with me.

He hammered hard, constructing the cage and situating it in the sand beyond the kitchen door. Chinquapin and his mother left him to his work, so that by dinnertime he had made a sturdy cage for his gull.

He put the sleek gray Jetser inside the cage that was six by six by six feet big. The bird flew around and around, frantic to be free, beating her beak against the wire until it bled.

Luke chided himself for his neglect. "Chinquapin!" he called. "I need you."

She came running. "What can I do?"

"Come seine for fish with me. Jetser is starved."

They each took one end of a net and waded into the water where the small fish flashed. They tugged and pulled and plunged deep. When they lifted the net it twinkled with shining bellies.

They carried them back and threw them to the frightened bird. Jetser walked gingerly toward them. Then swiftly, with powerful stabs of her beak, she ate thirty while Chinquapin counted.

For the next three days as July waned Luke watched the beach road expecting to see his father return home in wrath. But the gulls flew over it and the sandpipers ran down its wet edge. Shells sparkled on it. Luke worked on, copying his notes on Spacecraft, and getting his thoughts on paper for his friend, Dr. Allard.

On the last day of the month he mailed his proposal and notes as he had promised. Then he settled down to catch Spacecraft.

By going back over the notes of the past week, Luke found that every day around two o'clock Spacecraft came to the dump. There, he sat on a boiler. When the ferryboat from New London came into his view, he flew from the boiler to meet it. He rode into port on the mast, picked up a few pieces of bread from the passengers, then sailed across Great Pond to Block Island Bay. There he loafed.

That night Luke tapped on the wall between his loft and Chinquapin's. He could see that her light was on.

"I think I know how to trap Spacecraft," he said.

She opened the small door between their rooms.

The past week with her had been the nicest they had ever had. He decided that he liked his little sister. "How?" she asked respectfully.

"I'll set a snap net on that boiler in the dump where he sits every day. I called the Navy airport. A jet is due over the island tomorrow at two. When it zooms over, Spacecraft will jerk with fright. You'll be lying behind the icebox and will pull the string while I jump from behind the morris chair and catch him."

She laughed. "That'll be fun." She turned away.

"Chinquapin?"

"What?"

"Has mother gotten more letters from Dad?"

"Yes, two came today. Why?"

"What did he say? Did she tell you?"

"Oh, just that everything was going along fine, except that the 'hahaha' tapes weren't working."

Luke had forgotten all about the tapes and their failure; he had been so engrossed in his own problems. "You know," he suddenly said to Chinquapin, "maybe Dr. Allard will remember our family story and tell Dad to come home."

"What family story?"

"The one about how the gulls hate Dad. He could get a good tape here if he sacrificed himself to science."

Chinquapin laughed. "I'll say he could! Larus

would be the Sinatra of the bird recording world. What a hit *that* record would be."

She closed the door and the lights went out. Luke lay awake on his cot and thought about his father, and wondered for the hundredth time why he had not ordered him to come back to Boston. He could not understand.

At noon the next day Luke set the net trap on the boiler. He opened it until it lay like a butterfly—the spring treadle in the middle, the hooped nets on either side. On the treadle he tied a chicken leg—a gull favorite. Carefully he laid the trip cord over the boxes and iron and broken chairs to the icebox where Chinquapin would hide.

Then he went home for lunch. During the meal Luke occasionally glanced at his mother's face to see if there were anything there to tell him that his father was angry. Her face was happy and serene.

After lunch Chinquapin and Luke walked down the beach to the trap. Luke decided to explain his project to her. It pleased him that she listened excitedly to his plans. It seemed completely sensible to her for two birds afraid of jets to mate and then train their young to be afraid of jets also. Suddenly she stopped walking.

"But suppose they won't mate?" she asked. "Dad says they mate for life. Sea gulls don't like just *any* sea gull."

Luke walked on. "We'll just have to hope," he replied. But as couples go, they've sure got a lot in common."

"But it will take a long time to prove anything, won't it?"

"Years, maybe."

"And then will airports be safe?"

"I don't know. This is pure science, basic research. I have to find out if fear is taught or inherited in birds . . . that's all."

She stopped again. "Honestly, you're as bad as Dad. At least he's finally putting his knowledge to practical use. I even think he's glad to do it."

"He loves it," Luke said.

At the dump he crawled behind the chair and stood among springs and window frames. Chinquapin crouched behind the icebox and took hold of the string.

"When I say, 'Pull,' pull."

The brown curls disappeared behind the wind-beaten box. Luke went down into the ruins of the morris chair. Presently the soft "mew" cry of the gulls sang over the island. "All's well," they were saying as they crossed the grass hills to the dump. Some flapped steadily as they came. Others coasted on an updraft that bounced off the face of the dunes.

Closer and closer they came, drifting and talking

and riding the winds . . . to descend on the chairs and doors and oil drums.

One bird folded its wings like fans and alighted on the boiler, in the middle of the net. It began to pick at the food. Luke could feel his heart bounce against his ribs. He lifted his head and was about to shout to Chinquapin when he noticed the bands. It was the wrong bird! An ache of disappointment gripped him. He did not move.

The bird on the net ate all the chicken, then opened its wings. A breeze lifted it a few feet and it dropped on the edge of a door. Another gull cried above the boiler. It was Spacecraft. He was lowering his legs to alight . . . but not on the net.

He descended gracefully onto the top of an oil drum three feet from the trap. Luke was about to lunge at him in desperation when the jet came screaming overhead. For the moment Luke had forgotten it. He jumped in alarm as Spacecraft buckled and flopped behind the drum.

Luke lunged over the debris. The big wings flapped. Luke reached into a crevass between the drum and a box and took hold of the terrified bird. Spacecraft struggled mightily, and Luke held on for dear life.

Chinquapin screamed, "Shall I pull?"

"Get me a string!" Luke yelled. "Ouch! This bird bites like a tiger. Hurry!"

He stumbled over the debris, clutching Spacecraft, afraid he would trip and fall. The bird had a tight grip on his arm. Chinquapin had emerged from behind the icebox and was staring at him with her eyes wide and her mouth open. Finally she snapped to and pulled her handkerchief from her pocket. Fumbling, she tied the bird's beak tight. Luke threw back his head and laughed in spite of his wound. "Come on," he said. "Leave all the stuff here. We've got to get this crazy wonderful bird into the cage!"

They ran all the way back along the edge of the sea.

As Chinquapin opened the cage door, Luke took the handkerchief off the beak. He tossed in the bird, threw his arms around his sister, and cried, "Bravo! I make you honorary president of the 'What happened to Spacecraft Club.'"

The frightened bird flopped into a corner and stared at them. His eyes were wide, and he was panting with fear. Luke felt sorry for him. But his heart was high with a sense of accomplishment.

"Come on!" Chinquapin said. "Let's catch him some fish."

His elation rose higher as he followed her to the sea, dragging the seine as he ran.

They threw twenty small fish to the birds, then sat down behind the house to see if Spacecraft would eat. He huddled in the corner, refusing to move. Jetser stabbed the fish and ate them all with relish.

"I hope he doesn't give us that kind of trouble," Luke said. "It's terrible when a bird won't eat."

"Maybe he'd like to see a red spot on a lollipop so he could open his mouth," Chinquapin said in fun.

Luke looked at his sister in amazement. "You could be right," he said seriously, "You could be very right. He's pretty old for that kind of nonsense, but it's worth a try."

He ran to the lab for the lollipop cut-out his father had used in his experiments. How long ago that seemed.

Luke held the cut-out above the frightened bird. Spacecraft stared up at it, and seemed to relax a little. He pecked it. But his peck expressed anger more than affection.

"He's forgotten his childish ways," Chinquapin said. "Makes me realize there's a lot to know about gulls. Like when do baby gulls stop wanting to tap?"

An hour or so later, Spacecraft had completely relaxed. He stood up and preened. Luke and Chinquapin went back to the sea for more fish. They threw the fish into the cage, and watched happily as Spacecraft stepped resolutely toward the fish. Suddenly Chinquapin straightened and demanded, "Isn't that a whirlybird coming this way?" She pointed to the northwest.

Luke looked beyond her finger. "Looks like it. Probably one of the weather men."

'The helicopter came on. Luke squinted his eyes and peered at it. "Isn't it orange and green?"

"Yes, I think so. Why?"

"The president of Airways has an orange and green whirlybird," Luke said slowly. "I'll bet he's bringing Dad home." Apprehension filled him as he thought of their last words together.

Mr. David's whirlybird hovered right over the Sea Bird Lab, then dropped lightly onto the sand. Mrs. Rivers came up behind Luke and Chinquapin and watched with quiet wonder. "To think a month ago no one knew we existed on this sandspit with the gulls," she said.

Luke's father was the first to jump out. Next came Dr. Olsen. Three men followed, listing heavily with recording equipment.

Luke had an involuntary desire to go the other way. I ought to get that net, he thought. No, I'll show Dr. Olsen the gullery. That way I won't have to talk to Dad. He recognized his own cowardice and squared his shoulders. No . . . I'll face the music . . . and here it comes.

Luke stood in the background and watched his father introduce engineers and pilots, ornithologists and technicians to his mother and Chinquapin. He heard his mother say with a faint sound of desperation, "If someone will build a fire I'll make a pot of coffee." They reassured her. The whirlybird had its own kitchen. They took her and Chinquapin to see it.

Then Luke's father turned toward him. "Hi," his father said lightly. His voice gave away none of his feelings.

Luke took a deep breath. "I'm sorry I had to leave, Dad. I apologize. But I've captured Spacecraft."

"It was your decision," his father said. He did not smile. He did not frown. He seemed to mean what he said. "We're here because you told Dr. Allard how Larus screams at me." He smiled and winked. Luke took heart.

He couldn't hold back his next question. He needed the approval of this man he loved, and fought. "Then you aren't mad about Spacecraft?" No sooner was the question out than he knew he had gone too far. His father's face sobered immediately.

"You have asked me a question," his father said, in a low voice. "I shall answer it. My five-year study of gulls shows that the chick comes from the egg complete with deep instincts of behavior. I think you are very wrong. You have one strange bird—not hundreds." And he turned and walked swiftly toward the men with the equipment.

Luke dug his bare toes deeper and deeper into the sand. A great lump came up in his throat. He wanted to cry. He lifted his eyes to the sea, closed them, and said fiercely to himself, well, then, I'll prove I am wrong. That's science, too.

The afternoon was devoted to wiring the gullery for sound. A few birds still had young on Rebel and Yank hills, so Dr. Rivers was hopeful of rousing a strong alarm cry. He stayed in the lab while the others took care of the wiring, as he did not want any of the birds to see him until everything was ready.

Luke helped the engineers carry wires to the lighthouse. Because there was no electricity on that end of the island they plugged their equipment into the big batteries that lit the beacon.

Mr. David, who was enjoying the unusual afternoon away from the office, joined Luke and Dr. Olsen. He glanced at the white wings in the sky.

"They don't seem any nastier than the Boston gulls," he observed. Then he chuckled. "Want to bet our birds are meaner than your birds?"

"Yes," replied Luke. "There's no Boston bird as mad at anyone as Larus is at my father. Dad was nervous the day he banded him, and he must have scared the dickens out of him. After all, Larus was the first bird Dad had banded. Larus must have felt Dad's nervousness, and he responded. Animals are very sensitive to people's feelings, you know."

Neither man offered any comment, so Luke went

on, "Anyway, I think after Larus got to be president of the gulls he passed his anger on to others. I can come out here in August when the nesting season's done without a hat or raincoat . . . but not Dad."

"I can't really quite believe they dislike your father more than they do you or me or Mr. David," Dr. Olsen said.

Luke was so surprised he hardly knew what to say. "Don't you think gulls can tell one person from another?"

"Not to that point," Dr. Olsen said firmly.

"Heck," said Luke, "they can tell each other apart two or three miles away; a mere human face would be nothing to them."

"You can tell people apart, but you can't tell birds apart," Dr. Olsen said with condescension. "It would be nice if you could, then you wouldn't have to band them."

Luke did not want to argue. Time will argue for me, he said to himself. When Dad walks out on that gullery Dr. Olsen will wonder *why* the birds scream, not *if* they scream. He grinned privately. It was nice to feel confident again.

The engineers made the routine tests and then called, "We're ready!" They laughed. "Now where's the star?"

Now Luke was annoyed. No one in the party believed that these gulls would fuss louder at his father than at any other person in the world. He wondered why they had come if they were in such doubt.

"Dad!" he called. He hurried down the lighthouse dune and over the trail to the lab. Chinquapin rushed up from the water and their mother came outside from the kitchen. Here was solidarity. At least *we* all believe in Dad. He glanced back at Dr. Olsen and Mr. David, the engineers and the pilot. They were waiting tolerantly. You just wait, he thought grimly.

Dr. Rivers put on a black slicker, took a pith helmet, and started out. He checked his watch and said to Luke, "The time is right, isn't it?"

"Yes. Larus has been around the lighthouse every day at this time ever since I've been home."

"Well, he better not let us down today."

Dr. Rivers lifted his binoculars to study the gulls on the roof of the building. He paused as he focused, then smiled. "He's the one nearest the light," he said, and started walking toward the dune where the recording party waited.

"Some show," Luke's mother giggled. "I never thought I'd have a bird matinee idol for a husband."

Chinquapin giggled too, and folded her arms over her chest. "Our hero," she said. "Some kids watch their fathers get Best Citizen of the Year Awards, but not the Rivers children. They watch their father walk bravely across a dune, head high, chest out, to be screamed at by a gull."

Luke chuckled warmly at his sister and wiggled his shoulder a few inches closer to her as they leaned against the wall together. They waited in utter confidence.

Luke kept his eye on the lighthouse. The bird near the light grew nervous as the black figure walked toward Yank Hill. Several times he lowered his wings to fly, then thought better of it and relaxed.

"Go on!" Luke said aloud. He could see Dr. Olsen waiting with patient resignation against the lighthouse wall. His father walked on. The technical men were at their station, but not very alert.

Larus was now concentrating fully on the black figure. The bird pulled himself up tall and thin. Good, Luke thought. He's flattened his feathers to his body. He's scared.

"His wings are drooped," Chinquapin breathed excitedly.

Then with a thrust Larus dropped on his wings. Luke saw his father remove his helmet and take off his coat.

I hope he doesn't get hurt, Luke thought with a sudden pang.

And then Larus broke into a reverberating distress call. The air sounded with his "HA HA HA HA HA

HA HA!" His voice was so desperate that three other gulls began to scream, too. The noise was deafening.

Dr. Olsen straightened up. The men at the tape recording machine were so surprised that they fumbled their dials. The gulls were now circling and crying, and Luke could see that they were getting ready to strike their enemy. And his father was unprotected! The gulls folded their wings and plunged. Dr. Rivers' arms went up to cover his face and he dropped to the ground, as gulls ripped down on him.

Luke found himself running to help. He knew the wrath of the birds, even if Dr. Olsen did not. He got to the lighthouse just as the engineer threw up a handkerchief. "Okay! Come in! Cut!"

Dr. Rivers grabbed up the black raincoat and ran into the lighthouse, waving the helmet to fend off the birds. Luke could see a red gash on his forehead.

"Are you all right?" he demanded, out of breath from sprinting up the hill.

"Yes. Sure," his father said with a shrug. "It's not deep. How was it?"

"Splendid! Bravo!" called Dr. Olsen. "I can't believe it."

He rushed to shake Dr. Rivers' hand, his face beaming with delight. "You're marvelous. I think this will do the trick. Any gull who hears this tape is going to take off for China."

Luke looked at him and thought, there's one big

187

thing about a scientist that's a pleasure to see; he never minds being proved wrong.

The engineers came over to his father with renewed respect.

"This is the hottest record in the nation!" one of them said, and the laughter mingled with, "Haha-haha."

The Post Boat

The whirlybird was ready to depart early the next
morning. His father did not ask Luke to come back
with him. They would work apart from now on.
Luke walked as far as the pump, and watched the
great propellers whirl and spin and rise over the
surf to fly away. Chinquapin ran out to the very end
of the spit and waved her red scarf with her whole
body.

"I hope it's a hit! I hope it's a hit!" she called.

So be it, said Luke and picked up the seine to get
fish for his birds.

As he passed the cage he stopped to study them.

They were accustomed to confinement now, but not
to each other. Spacecraft kept a red-rimmed eye on
the female. Occasionally he felt hostile toward her
and lowered his wings. This would prompt her to
walk in small circles.

There's so much to know, Luke said to himself.
What they were doing at that moment was a puzzler.
But he would have to begin somewhere. So he would
begin where his father taught him—with notes.

He went into the lab and worked out a chart. Each
morning at seven and again at two, he would weigh
the birds. At eight and three he would make notes of
what they were doing for fifteen minutes at a time.

A year of this and I should begin to know something about these creatures, he thought as he labo-
riously drew a chart for each day of the year.

When the work was done he went to the window
and called to Chinquapin.

"Come to town with me. I've got an idea." Chinquapin sat up, hesitated a moment, and then ran to
him. As her feet tossed up the sand Luke wondered
at this girl who was his sister. She likes to please, he
thought. She likes to be liked. I used to fight with
her. Now I see she is really a warm little person, who
will someday have cozy little girls of her own.

She was beside him, straight-legged and alert.
"What are you going to do?"

"I'm going to town to call the Navy base and see
if I can't find out when all the jets fly over Block

Island. Then I can fill in the last column of my chart
—what Spacecraft does when the jets go over."

"I think he'll forget and grow up to be a sensible
gull." She smiled up at him as they walked the beach.
"But I think you should find out."

Luke kicked a shell. "I think I should find out, too.
I don't know why, cause I'm probably dead wrong.
But I just seem to have to."

"I know why."

"You do?"

"Because you're mad at Dad and want to say 'See,
I told you so.'"

"I guess I felt that way earlier in the summer,
when I tried to get a fellowship. I wanted everyone to
look at me and say, 'There goes a famous scientist.'"
Luke smiled at the remembrance. "But I don't feel
that way anymore. I really want to know why Spacecraft hides when he hears the scream of jets, and I
want to see if he can pass that behavior on to his
children. I've got to know for *myself*."

"Well, let's find out, then," she said. She ran ahead,
then turned and came back. "Got any money? I want
a sundae."

"You know I don't have any money. You're the
millionaire."

"But you earned some in Boston, didn't you?"

"I didn't get paid. I quit and in Dad's terms, I
forfeited the money."

"Wow! That father of ours. He's an iron-fist where

money is concerned." She angrily scuffed the sand as she walked. "You know what he did? Banked my money. He put all that good spending money in a bank!"

"Oh, well," Luke shrugged. "You don't have to have money to be happy. There's nothing I want right now. And you'll get fat if you eat a sundae."

"You sound like Dad. Making up nice reasons for being miserable."

She leaned down and picked up a round stone. Luke watched her throw it into the white waves. He was amused to see that she threw like a girl. He wondered why girls always got their elbows and heads in the way of a good toss. He decided he liked it on a girl. It made her look helpless.

Suddenly he found himself wondering how Ginny threw a stone. He imagined with contentment that she threw just like his sister. The thought warmed him.

They biked down the road to Old Harbor. Luke borrowed Captain Gregory's telephone and called the Navy base. The officer on duty gave him the departure time for three daily jets. The rest were classified, he told Luke . . . secret.

As Luke hung up the telephone, the Block Island gulls gathered above the breakwater, circling and calling their plaintive "mew." He walked to the fishhouse window to see why they were gathering. Then he realized what day it was. Abnormality used to feed them at this hour every Tuesday. Luke's sadness was immediately replaced by wonder. Did the gulls know the days of the week? Did they have a sense of time? He ran out the lobster shack and over the wharf. At the end of the pier he jammed to a stop. Ginny and Chinquapin were throwing bread to the birds.

He started up again as swiftly as he had stopped and jumped over the rocks to join them. "What are you doing?" he called.

"I feed the gulls every Tuesday since Abnor is gone," Ginny said with a smile. "I figure they got used to it."

Luke laughed and turned to go back to the shack. Suddenly he remembered—spun around to watch Ginny throw the bread. She yanked her hand hard in at her side, like a boy. But when she let go, her elbow and head got in the way of each other. He laughed. It was all right on Ginny, too.

For the next week Luke worked hard. Spacecraft went into panic at every jet flight, and Jetser hid under a box. As the days passed Jetser seemed to be growing used to the noisy flights, but Spacecraft was as frightened as ever.

I must have really damaged his spirit, Luke thought as he watched his bird and remembered the long-ago day when he dropped the chick.

The lazy days at the end of the summer all seemed

alike. They were filled with work, play, swimming, and an occasional movie with Chinquapin and Ginny. Time was Luke's. It gave him a sense of well being.

After his father departed Luke and Chinquapin had eagerly waited to hear how the tape worked. No word came. Luke thought his father was too busy to write. Chinquapin said he was probably dickering with the postman over the price of a stamp. Finally, after five days, a telegram arrived. The messenger boy had not been able to find the Sea Bird Lab!

But even late, the word was still news. His mother read aloud,

"We wowed them in Boston!"

A letter followed the telegram. Dr. Rivers wrote that the gull tape was a sensation and that copies were being made for other airports. He added, "Dr. Olsen has gone home to Philadelphia to get a starling as mad at him as Larus was at me. He wants to make tapes of starling distress calls. These birds are much more of a problem at airports than gulls." Then he added that he would be home on August 16th and wanted everyone to be packed to go home. The following day they would leave for Columbus. School was to start early in September.

On the afternoon of August 16th Luke walked to Old Harbor to meet his father. The sun was hot. He sat quietly on a piling as the boat came in. A few gulls accompanied the ferry into the slip, but it was so warm that most of them were rocking on the waves, resting from the heat.

Dr. Rivers drove the beach wagon down the gangplank and Luke hopped in. "How's Spacecraft?" his father asked.

Luke was pleased and a little relieved. "He's eating quite well now, but he's still afraid of Jetser. She's an awful bossy female. I don't think they'll ever make a go of their marriage. All she has to do is lift her head and Spacecraft acts like a scared child."

"The winter months and the increasing light of January and February should take care of that." Dr. Rivers smiled. "The rhythm of the seasons soothes the fights between male and female birds."

"I guess you're right," Luke answered. "Besides, Spacecraft is nice. She ought to like him. She ought to be glad to let him lift his head above her."

"She will."

They pulled up beside the Sea Bird Lab. Luke watched his father step out of the car and stand a moment, smelling the salty wind from the ocean. He seemed to move his heart into the house, the sandspit, and the sky.

"I'm going to miss this place," he said.

Luke's heart sank. Why hadn't he thought of this? "We aren't coming back next year?"

"No. The work is done. Besides, I am suddenly an

applied scientist. I have requests to go to European airports and to western and southern United States, and an airline in India has asked me to come help them. I may have to get a leave from the University."

"You mean you're going to give up basic research?"

"I'm more useful putting my knowledge to work right now." Luke detected a sadness in his father's voice. He felt pain, too, as he realized that the long hard hours of work, the lonely assignments, were over. There had been much that was beautiful about it. But now the Rivers family had to join the stream of humanity. People needed his father. For the first time in his life Luke was not sure he wanted to go with the crowd.

He carried his father's briefcase to the lab. His mother hugged her husband warmly.

"I'm so proud of you," she said. "To think that you and Larus are a big success." Then she added, "So big, that we've outgrown the Sea Bird Lab." She stood back and looked at him. "I don't think I'm going to like you in Bowler hats instead of pith helmets," she said.

At noon the next day Dr. Rivers told Luke to stop packing. He said they just couldn't make the two o'clock ferry. None of them could complete their last-minute jobs. Chinquapin couldn't possibly feel the sand between her toes in two hours. Luke's mother couldn't walk along the beach in so short a time.

Luke sat down on the boxes and suitcases and shook his head. "We're all completely mad," he said. "Which is a good thing, because we can't notice it in each other."

His father picked up a hammer and a nail and started to repair a loose board on the floor.

"Come on," Luke said, "that's going too far. Let's walk in for the mail."

They followed the beach around the island, their binoculars swinging around their necks. Occasionally they checked a bird, but mostly they just ambled and looked at the sky and sea. They did not talk at all. Luke was bursting with the happiness of the place.

At Old Harbor they passed the time of day with Captain Gregory, and stood with the fishermen and tourists, staring at a beautiful new game boat that was tied at the wharf.

"Joining the crowd isn't so bad," his father said. "It's fun to do nothing but stare at a boat." He stepped on the deck and peered in the cabin, then jumped off.

They followed the mail car to the post office. There were letters for his father from all over the world. Several were from Boston, two from Alaska, and one from Washington. And there was one for Luke, but it looked like an ad so he did not open it until they were on the road going home. Then casually he pulled out the letter.

"Dad," he said very quietly, "this is from Dr. Allard." He was silent while he read. "He submitted the outline of my study to the National Science Foundation. They are considering it for a fellowship to college. I. . . ." But Luke could not go on. He swatted a mosquito on his face with a powerful blow, regained his composure, and said, "And here's a check for $200 for equipment to keep the birds this winter. It's Dr. Allard's personal check."

The wind came off the ocean and fluttered the papers in Luke's hand. His father had stopped walking.

"Luke," he said, "that's a fine tribute."

Over the green hills of Block Island a gull flew. Its white wings were spread motionless against the sky as it peered down on the island below. Then plaintively it called, "Meeeeeew."

Dr. Rivers squinted up at the beautiful white sea gull. "All's well in our world, too," he sang out. And the bird flew on.

ABOUT THE AUTHOR

The enthusiastic reception that young people accord each new book by Jean George is seconded by their parents, teachers, and librarians. Mrs. George is coauthor of *Dipper of Copper Creek,* which received the Aurianne Award for the most outstanding animal story published in 1957. *My Side of the Mountain* and *The Summer of the Falcon* both affirmed her remarkable sensitivity to the world of nature and of people.

Mrs. George is a regular contributor of nature stories to *Reader's Digest.* She has held the position of art editor for *Pageant* magazine and has served as a newspaper reporter for the Washington *Post* and International News Service.

She lives with her three children in Chappaqua, New York.